GUY TIME

SARAH WEEKS

W9-CAW-617

A LAURA GERINGER BOOK

HarperTrophy®
An Imprint of HarperCollinsPublishers

Harper Trophy® is a registered trademark of HarperCollins Publishers Inc.

Guy Time
Copyright © 2000 by Sarah Weeks

Library of Congress Cataloging-in-Publication Data
Weeks, Sarah.
    Guy time / Sarah Weeks.
        p.   cm.
    Sequel to: Regular Guy.
    Summary: A humorous account of thirteen-year-old Guy's dealing with the separation, and
possible divorce, of his eccentric parents and with his own newfound interest in girls.
    ISBN 0-06-028365-3. — ISBN 0-06-028366-1 (lib. bdg.) — ISBN 0-06-440783-7 (pbk.)
    [1. Parent and child—Fiction.] I. Title.
PZ7.W42235Gu   2000   99-36856
[Fic]—dc21   CIP
                                                                          AC

Typography by Al Cetta
❖
First Harper Trophy edition, 2001
Visit us on the World Wide Web!
www.harperchildrens.com

To my sweet son Natty

—S.W.

CHAPTER ONE

"It's embarrassing; that's what it is," I said to Buzz as we walked home after soccer practice. "And she just keeps doing it."

"Who is she going out with this time, Guy?" he asked.

"His name is Brad, and when I asked her what he does for a living she told me he's 'in fur.'"

"What does that mean—'in fur'? Does he wear it?" asked Buzz.

"I think it means he sells it," I said.

"You mean like a Good Humor man would be in *ice cream*?" Buzz asked as he kicked the soccer ball ahead of him on the sidewalk.

"I guess," I said.

"Where's *Brad* taking her?" Buzz asked.

"I don't want to know," I said. I tapped the ball away from Buzz with my foot and kicked it hard up onto Mr. Biedermeyer's lawn. "Probably a mink farm."

The ball shot across the grass and rolled out of sight under a big rhododendron bush. "Hang on a sec," I said, and went to retrieve it.

My life has never been exactly what you'd call normal, but ever since my parents split up six months ago, and my mother started going out on dates with guys like Brad, it's been especially freaky.

I'm a regular thirteen-year-old kid by most people's standards, but my parents, Lorraine and William "Wuckums" Strang, are both on the odd side. Well, at least my mother is. My father *used* to be odd but now he's normal, which, I guess, when you think about it, is kind of odd in itself. The same man who only a year ago was walking around Cedar Springs in high-water pants, white socks, and penny loafers now wears designer suits and gets a manicure once a week. Sometimes I barely recognize him.

It's all on account of his work. My father is "into" computers. I used to think that meant he was always up to his elbows in gears and sprockets and microchips, pulling wires out of the backs of monitors like some sort of mad scientist. Now I know that what he does is invent software programs that do stuff for people who are sick and tired of having to do stuff for themselves.

He didn't use to have to dress up and have clean fingernails to do his work, but then he invented TLC and everything changed. He traveled all over the country for conferences. Then he started going off to places like Japan and Germany for weeks at a time. He was making a lot more money than he ever had before. We got a new car and a refrigerator that shoots ice and two different kinds of cold drinks out of holes in the front of the door. Well, at least it used to shoot drinks, before my mother filled it with kefir, this gross runny yogurt stuff. That pretty much gummed it up for good, but it still shoots ice.

Having more money in the family was the good part about my dad's new job. The bad part was that after TLC became a household word, something rotten happened in *my* household: My mom and dad stopped getting along.

It's not like it was so unusual for my parents to fight. They'd always done it, but this was different. Usually they did junk like yell stuff at each other and slam doors, and every now and then one of them would stomp off somewhere in a huff.

Like one time my mother got really mad at my dad about something and flew off to a yoga retreat in California without telling us where she was going. She stayed there for about a week while my dad and I hung out and ate her entire stockpile of frozen low-fat dinners. When she finally came home, all she wanted to do was play this touchy-feely music and walk around the house in a turban chanting, "I am serene, I am serene. . . ." It was a little creepy, but I was glad she was home, and after a couple of days she and my father made up, and life went back to normal. Well, as normal as it ever was around my house.

But after my dad changed, my parents started having fights that lasted for days. Sometimes at dinner they wouldn't look at each other. Once in the middle of an argument I heard my father say: "Lorraine, it's high time you grew up."

She responded by throwing a big fat grapefruit at his head. He ducked, and it broke a pane in the kitchen window. A lot of times one or the other of them would be asleep on the couch when I got up in the morning.

Then one day, about six months ago, my dad packed a suitcase. At first I thought he was just taking another business trip, but then he asked me to come sit on the porch with him, and he put his arm around me and told me that he was moving out. I couldn't believe it.

"Maybe you and Mom just need a little break from each other," I said. "Buzz and I do that sometimes. Just take a little break from each other until things blow over."

He shook his head and didn't say anything.

My dad moved to San Diego, temporarily, to help train people at some huge company that was installing TLC in every computer in the joint. He sent me a photo of the condo they put him up in. It had a red tile roof and a big pool in the back and tall palm trees all around it. He called me all the time, pretty much every day. He said I could come visit anytime I wanted to, but I figured he'd be home soon enough so why bother to fly all the way out there and miss school and get jet lag? I was sure he'd come back before long, but after five months he was still out in

California. It was around that time that my mother dropped the big bomb.

"I've got to start thinking about making a new life for myself," she said one day.

"What's the matter with the life you've got now?" I asked.

"I'm lonely," she said.

"Oh," I said, hoping she wasn't about to suggest that we spend more time together. I love my mother, but she's best in small doses.

"I put a personal ad in the paper," she went on, "and I've gotten several interesting responses already. I'm a little nervous about it, but I've agreed to meet one of them, Henry Blankman, this afternoon."

Henry Blankman. It rang a bell.

"Wait a second. *Mr. Blankman*, the science teacher at my school? Are you crazy, Mom? You can't go out on a date with my science teacher. That's sick."

"We're only going to a movie," she said as she put on her lipstick and smacked her lips together on a Kleenex. "He sounded nice on the phone. What does he look like, anyway?"

I was in a panic. This couldn't be happening.

"He's bald as an egg, but that's not the point, Mom. Don't you get it? You can't go out on a date! Not with Mr. Blankman. Not with anyone. In case you've forgotten, you're *married to Dad!* Besides being beyond disgusting, it's illegal for you to go out on a date, isn't it?" I shouted.

"Your father and I are legally separated now, Guy," she said softly.

I didn't say anything. I couldn't. I felt like someone had punched me in the stomach and I couldn't catch my breath. "Legally separated." I didn't like the sound of that one bit.

"The papers just came through last week," she said. "Willy Copley's father is our mediator. It's very amicable."

"Amicable?" I said.

"Friendly. We're not fighting about anything, your dad and I."

"If you're not fighting anymore, why doesn't he just come home?" I asked.

"It's not that simple, Guysie," she said as she touched my cheek with the back of her hand. Even though it wasn't supposed to, her touching me like that made me feel worse.

I stood there watching my mother scratch with her fingernail at a lipstick stain on one of her front teeth. The whole world seemed to be moving in slow motion somehow. Then the doorbell rang, and she put on her blue coat, the one my father gave her for Christmas last year. She kissed me on the cheek, or rather near my cheek on account of the lipstick, told me she loved me, and went downstairs to greet my dorky bald science teacher, her *date*, at the door.

There have been several times in my life when I've wondered if it's all some sort of cruel joke. The day Mr. Blankman took my mother to the movies was definitely one of them.

CHAPTER TWO

"How does it work, anyway, Guy?" asked Buzz. "Do you sit on the couch in your bathrobe and slippers waiting up for her when she goes out on one of her dates?"

"Yeah, right," I snorted as I groped around under the bush trying to get ahold of the ball. "You've been watching too many corny sitcoms. I don't even own a bathrobe and slippers."

"Well, what would you do if you opened the door and she and some guy were out there on the porch, like, *kissing* or something?" Buzz asked.

"Quit bugging me and help me get this freepin' ball out from under here, will you?"

My mother has been dating now for about a month. I can't say I'm exactly used to it yet, but I'm what you might call resigned to it. There's really nothing I can do about it. At least she and Mr. Blankman didn't hit it off. She came home alone right after the movie that day and said something like "He's not my cup of punch."

I'm glad she wasn't into him, because it would have been totally weird for me if they'd decided to go steady, or whatever adults do when they like each other.

Until my mother started going out, I had no idea how many weirdos there are in the world. Like Stan the ferret man, for instance. He brought his stinky little pet weasel with him everywhere he went. My mom told me he asked her to stash it in her purse when they went into the restaurant, but she made him take it back out and leave it in the car. After him came the "I only eat green food" guy, and then Harry the Kazoo King. His claim to fame? He could play three kazoos at the same time—one in his mouth and one in each nostril. All I could think about was: What if he got them mixed up in between concerts? Yech.

Ever since the dating began, I have been haunted by the thought that my mother might divorce my father and decide to marry one of these geeky types she's been dating. I know she has a soft spot for unusual men—after all, she married my dad, and he was about as offbeat as they come. I'm sure on the inside he still is. I mean, just because you buff your fingernails and know how to tie a Windsor knot in your necktie doesn't mean your whole personality changes. At least I don't think it does.

My dad's favorite trick, the thing he was probably most famous for before he invented TLC, was to snort a raw oyster up his nose and spit it out his mouth. Who knows, maybe when he and the other businessmen he hangs out with now are cutting loose in the boardroom, he does it for them. It's a little hard to picture, but I kind of hope he still does it every now and then.

There are a lot of things I hope, like that my parents will get back together, and even though my mother is still wacky and my father is a straight arrow, they'll remember that they used to be crazy about each other.

What I don't like to think about is how my life will be if my parents end up getting divorced for real and my dad stays in California and my mom hooks up with the ferret man and we all have to live under the same roof—me and Mom and the beady-eyed weasel—

"Earth to Guy. Earth to Guy."

"Huh?" I said, suddenly coming to my senses.

"What are you doing lying under here in the dirt like a bug, Guy? I thought you were trying to get the ball," Buzz said as he crawled farther under the bush and looked at me up close. "You okay?"

"Yeah. I'm just thinking," I said.

"Thinking is generally a good thing, Guy Wire, but not when you're lying under a bush trying to get a soccer ball while your best friend in the whole world is starving to death and has to pee so bad his teeth are floating."

"Sorry, Buzzard. Here, take this stick and poke the ball at the same time I do, only do it from the other side, okay?"

After a few clumsy attempts, we finally managed to pin the ball between us like a big white dumpling in a pair of chopsticks, and then on the count of three we pulled it out from under the bush and sent it shooting out onto the lawn.

"All reetie, baked ziti!" shouted Buzz as we ran after the ball.

The two of us passed it back and forth in silence the rest of the way to my house.

CHAPTER THREE

"**A**nybody home?" I called as we came in the back door.

There was no answer, so I figured my mother was out doing errands or something. Buzz made a beeline for the bathroom, or "the facilities," as he sometimes calls it, and I went into the kitchen. There was a pot of thick reddish-pink stuff simmering on the stove. It smelled like strawberries. Probably a pie filling or something. My mother likes to bake. I dipped a wooden spoon into the mixture and stuck it in my mouth just as my mother walked into the kitchen in her robe with her wet hair wound up in a towel.

"Don't eat that!" she screamed.

I had just swallowed a big mouthful of it, and visions of an ambulance ride to the hospital to have my stomach pumped danced before my eyes as I dropped the spoon and rushed spluttering to the sink, scraping frantically at my tongue with my fingernails. Buzz came running into the kitchen.

"Should I call nine-one-one? What did he eat, Mrs. Strang? Was it rat poison?" he shouted as he raced across the room and grabbed for the phone.

"Stop!" my mother hollered. "It's not rat poison, for heaven's sake. It's my strawberry–kiwi–peach-fuzz fountain-of-youth facial lotion. It took me all day to make. Darn it, Guy, how much of it did you eat?"

"Just one spoonful," I answered. "I gotta say it tasted pretty good."

"Can I try it?" asked Buzz.

"No," said my mother. She picked up the wooden spoon, rinsed it off, and began stirring the mixture in the pot on the stove.

"This stuff is supposed to make my skin look ten years younger."

"If it doesn't work, can we have it for dessert tonight?" I said.

"Very funny. If you're hungry, why don't you have some snicker doodles? They're in the cookie jar," she said.

I opened the cookie jar and peered in. "It's empty," I said.

"Whoops," she said. "I meant to make more this morning, but I got kind of caught up in, well . . ."

"Getting dolled up for your big date with *Brad*," I said, letting my voice blat out his name like a foghorn. "What time is *Brad* picking you up?"

"Six o'clock. And don't start with me about Brad," my mother said defensively. "Who knows? Maybe he's the man of my dreams. I have to keep an open mind."

"Well, I don't," I said.

"You could try to be a little more supportive, Guy," my mother said.

"Okay, how's this for a helpful hint? If you're trying to impress the fur man, forget about coating your face with strawberries and go out in the yard and shoot a couple of squirrels to wear around your neck tonight," I said.

My mother stuck her tongue out at me and went back to stirring. Buzz laughed, and I pulled him by his sleeve out of the kitchen and up the stairs to my room.

"You wouldn't think it was so funny if it was *your* mother going out on a date, Buzzard," I said as I flopped down on the bed.

"Who would go out on a date with my mother?" Buzz asked. "Other than my father, I mean."

"Hopefully, you won't ever have to find out," I said.

"You never know. I *think* my parents still like each other, but that's what you thought too, right?"

"Yeah," I said.

"Have you heard from your dad lately?"

Buzz asked, kicking off his sneakers and settling in his usual spot on the end of my bed.

"Yeah, he sent me a photograph yesterday. Wanna see?" I asked, rummaging around in my night-table drawer, "Here." I handed him the photo.

"Sheesh," said Buzz as he took in the sight of my father in a three-piece suit standing in front of his condo. "I still can't get used to it. Wuckums is a businessman. Look, he's even got tassels on his shoes! Hey, how come he doesn't wear glasses anymore?"

"Contact lenses," I said, taking back the photo and shoving it in the drawer.

"Which one do you like better, the old version of your dad or the new one?" Buzz asked.

"I don't know. In a way the old one was annoying, but at least he was around to be annoyed with," I said.

"Do you think he's ever going to come back?" Buzz asked.

"I used to think so, but now, to tell you

the truth, I'm not so sure. I told you, they're legally separated, right? That's practically the same thing as being divorced," I said as I stretched out on the bed with my arms crossed behind my head.

"The important word there is *practically*. That means it's not a done deal yet. Have you told him you want him to come home?" asked Buzz.

"Sure," I said. "A bunch of times. He says he misses me like crazy, but he never says anything definite about coming back."

"Do you think your mother wants him to come back?" he asked.

"How would I know?" I said.

"Well, does it *seem* like she wants him to come back?" asked Buzz. "I mean, does she mope around and look all unhappy and stuff?"

"My mother never mopes. She's a *serene* person. Remember?" I said.

"Oh, right, 'I am serene, I am serene. . . .'" Buzz chanted in a high-pitched voice as he walked around the room with his arms stretched out in front of him as if he were in a trance.

"Yeah, serenity is just one of her many annoying personality traits," I said.

"Listen, it could be worse. Here's my mother: 'I am a fussbudget, I am a fussbudget. . . .' I'll take serenity over fussbudgetry any day," said Buzz.

"At least your mother acts her age," I said. "Mine acts like she thinks she's *my* age."

"She's not still talking about getting a tattoo, is she?" Buzz asked.

"No, but yesterday she mentioned something about having her navel pierced."

"Get out!" said Buzz.

"Get in!" I replied. "I think her whole idiotic thing about acting young is what drove my father to leave. He couldn't take it anymore."

"You think?" said Buzz.

"I *know*," I said. "I heard him tell her it was time for her to grow up."

"Oh, yeah. That's when she threw the papaya," said Buzz.

"Grapefruit," I corrected.

"Right. It's sad, you know, 'cause I always used to think your folks were like salt and pepper shakers," said Buzz.

"Huh?" I said.

"Like the ones my mom collects. You've seen them; they're on the shelf in the dining room. She has, like, two dogs—a big black salt-shaker dog with white spots and then a little white pepper shaker dog with black spots. They look cute together. Your folks were sort of like that—a matched set."

"Not anymore," I said.

"Yeah, remember that night they were going out to dinner with his boss and your mom put on that skirt made out of the paper birthday-party tablecloth?"

"Unfortunately, I do remember," I said. "They had a mondo fight about that."

"Does your mom ever talk about your dad?" asked Buzz.

"Not much, actually. A lot of times if I bring it up, she kind of changes the subject. I think it makes her uncomfortable."

"Why?"

"She probably feels guilty about driving him away by doing stupid stuff like wearing tablecloths," I said.

"I wonder if she misses him," Buzz asked.

"She's never said she does, but once when she was on the phone with her friend Wendy, I noticed that she was doodling my dad's name all over the back of the phone book."

"That could be significant," said Buzz, sitting up suddenly. "Doodling is supposed to be your unconscious mind speaking."

"Really?" I said.

"Yeah, so that means he's on her mind. She probably wishes he would come home, but she just doesn't know how to get him to do it. Maybe you should step in and help her," said Buzz.

"Help her how?" I asked as I sat up a bit

and leaned on one elbow to look at him.

"Like, if she can't get it together to tell him to come back, maybe you should tell him *for* her," said Buzz.

"What do you mean, tell him *for* her?" I asked.

"I mean, like pretend to be her and write him a letter, or something," said Buzz. "Isn't there a famous book about someone who does that? Some ugly guy with a big nose who writes great love letters for some handsome guy with a little nose who can't write worth beans?"

"I don't know about that, but I don't think writing a letter is such a hot idea," I said. "For one thing, I don't even know for sure if my mom wants my dad to come back. She's pretty into this dating thing now."

"Yeah, but she hasn't met anybody she likes yet, right? And don't forget about the phone-book doodling. She wasn't writing Brad's name all over it, was she?"

"No," I said.

"See? Come on, I'm sure she wants your dad to come home. She just needs some help, is all."

"I don't know. . . ."

"Well, don't you think it's worth a try? Listen, what if your mom ends up falling for Brad and they decide to get married? Picture it—the theme of the wedding is *fur*, so you have to walk her down the aisle and she's wearing, like, a big fur dress with a fur veil and you're wearing a beaver-pelt tuxedo and one of those great big fuzzy hats with ear-flaps. You don't want to risk that, do you?" said Buzz.

Just then the phone rang.

"Guy, it's for you!" my mother called up the stairs. "It's a *girl*!"

CHAPTER FOUR

"**T**hanks for sharing that piece of personal information with the whole world!" I called back as I rolled my eyes and reached for the phone.

Buzz watched with great interest.

"Yeah?" I said into the receiver.

"Guy? This is Autumn Hockney. Um, from Latin class?" said the soft, sweet voice on the other end of the line.

"Uh-huh," I said, and cringed as my voice cracked and leaped up an octave, making me sound like some goofy cartoon character. That had been happening to me a lot lately, especially when I was nervous. This was probably the first time I'd spoken to a girl on the phone since kindergarten, when I thought girls were the same as boys only with longer hair.

"Are you still there?" she asked.

"Yeah," I said.

"You do know who I am, right?" she said.

"I think so," I said, trying to control my voice.

I knew who she was, all right. She was the girl I stared at in Latin class because when she leaned over her book, her hair fell into her face and then she had this way of flipping it back over her shoulder which for some reason I found absolutely fascinating. Buzz was mouthing, "Who is it?" with big rubber-lipped exaggeration, but I waved the question away and listened to Autumn.

"Um, well, a bunch of us are going to the movies next weekend, and I was, uh, wondering if, um, you would like to, like, uh, go with me, Guy." She finally got it all out.

Had I heard that right? Had Autumn Hockney just asked me to go to the movies with her? I felt myself blush. Buzz was frantic by now, trying to figure out what was going on. I had no idea what to say to Autumn. Did I *want* to go to the movies with her? I didn't know. I took a deep breath and hoped whatever I said wouldn't sound too stupid.

"Uh, maybe," I said. "I'll let you know."

"Okay. Great. Well, 'bye," she said.

"'Bye," I said, and hung up the phone.

"I'm gonna bust a gut if you don't tell me who that was right now!" shouted Buzz, pushing me down on the bed and pounding on my chest with both his fists.

"It was Autumn Hockney," I said, not quite able to look him in the eye.

"*Autumn Hockney?* You mean the Hockney Puck?" Buzz said, getting off the bed and flopping into the chair by the window. "Gross. No wonder you looked so shocked. You're all red, you know. What did that holey old sock want?"

For some reason I couldn't bring myself

to tell Buzz that Autumn had sort of asked me to go to the movies with her. I knew I'd never hear the end of it, and besides, I wasn't sure how I felt about it yet. I needed some time to think.

"What did she want?" Buzz asked again.

"She needs help with her Latin," I said quickly, and I felt an instant pang of guilt for lying to my best friend.

"That's not the only kind of help she needs. What a dweeb. All she does is sit around flipping her stupid old hair. You ever notice that?" Buzz did a mean imitation of Autumn's hair flip.

"Nope. I never noticed," I said quietly, feeling another pang of guilt as I lied to Buzz for a second time in less than a minute.

Just then my mother stuck her head in the door. Buzz jumped about a mile. Her face, except for her lips and eyelids, was covered with the strawberry facial stuff, and her frizzy red hair was wrapped around two coffee cans, which she'd attached to her hair with long bobby pins. She looked like a Martian.

"Who was that, Guysie?" she asked.

"Nobody," I said.

"Exactly," agreed Buzz with a snort. "Nobody."

CHAPTER FIVE

"o you want me to stay until the fur guy comes to pick up your mom?" Buzz asked me at about five thirty.

"If you want," I said.

"I have to admit, I'd sort of like to check him out," said Buzz.

"Don't get your hopes up—I doubt if he's going to be wearing a leopardskin jumpsuit or anything," I said.

"That would be great, wouldn't it?" he said.

"Not really," I said with a heavy sigh.

Buzz patted me on the back a couple of times. I knew he hadn't meant to bum me out. We'd been best friends ever since he'd moved up to Cedar Springs from the South back in second grade. Actually, at the very beginning, when we first met, we hadn't hit it off right away because I thought he was nothing more than this polite little do-gooder who carried a handkerchief and said corny stuff like "Thank you kindly, ma'am." But once I got beyond his southern manners and discovered he had a lot more to him than that—some of it pretty grubby and impolite—I liked him just fine. He was funny most of the time, bossy some of the time, but always a true-blue friend when it came right down to it. Besides, he understood me better than anyone else in the world.

"I'm sorry, Guy," he said. "I didn't mean to make you feel bad, but do you have any idea how much more exciting it is around here than it is at my house? My parents are always saying stuff like 'Pass the potatoes, would you, please?' and 'It's time to put the storm windows in, dear, don't you think?'"

"Yeah, well, last fall when it was time to

put the storm windows in, my dad wasn't around to do it," I said. "And that's not exciting, that's a drag, because my mom and I both stink at that kind of stuff, and the windows leaked and rattled all winter."

Buzz looked at me for a minute, and I knew there was something he wanted to say but wasn't sure that he should. Then he went ahead and said it:

"Okay, I'm going out on a limb here, I know, but I'm gonna come right out and say what I gotta say, Guy. Quit moaning about your dad being gone and do something about it. He's not going to come back if you just sit around waiting for your mom to ask him to come home. Adults are pathetically slow; everybody knows that. You've gotta make a move. Write that letter from your mom."

"I don't know—"

"Well, *I* do. Why are you making such a big deal about this? Get me some paper," Buzz said.

I got some notebook paper out of the drawer and handed it halfheartedly to Buzz. He took the paper and shook his head.

"This stuff is fine for the first draft, but we're gonna need some of your mom's personal stationery for the final letter," he said. "Can you get your hands on some?"

"Oh great, now I'm impersonating her *and* stealing from her," I said as I sat back down on the bed.

"It's for a good cause," Buzz said. He grabbed a pencil and got ready to write. "Okay, first of all, what does she call him?"

"Wuckums," I said. "Everybody calls him that."

"'Dear Wuckums,'" wrote Buzz.

"No. Wait a second," I said. "I don't think she'd call him that right off the bat. That's what she calls him when they're getting along. She'd probably be more formal."

"Like what? 'Dear Mr. Strang?'" asked Buzz.

"No, you horsefly, like 'Dear William,'" I said.

"Fine. 'Dear William,'" wrote Buzz. "Now what?"

"I don't know. This was your idea. What do you think she'd say?" I asked.

"Well, it wouldn't be anything mushy, right? I mean, they must be mad at each other; otherwise your dad wouldn't have left. Usually people who are fighting talk all snotty. You know what I mean?" Buzz said.

"Yeah, but what's the point of being snotty if what we're trying to do is get him to come home?" I said.

"Good point. So maybe she'd say something about you, like 'I know you'll be happy to hear that our son, Guy, is doing just fine.'"

"That doesn't sound like her," I said.

"What does she sound like?" asked Buzz.

Just then my mother called to me from the bathroom. "Guysie-Pysie, bring me a couple of thingamadoodles from the box on my dresser, will you, hon bun?"

"She sounds like *that*," I said as I got up and went to get her a couple of Q-Tips from her room. Q-Tips are thingamadoodles, hair-pins are thingamabobs, and everything else is a thingamawhozit.

"This is harder than I thought," said Buzz when I came back into the room.

"Maybe we should figure out what we want to say first, and then worry about putting it into words that sound like my mother," I suggested.

"Good thinking," said Buzz.

We were interrupted by the doorbell at that point. I looked at the clock. Six o'clock—the fur man was right on time.

CHAPTER SIX

"**C**an you get that please, Guy?" my mother called from the bathroom.

"No way!" I called back in horror.

"Come on, Guychick. I've only got one eyelash on. What kind of impression am I going to make all unbalanced like that?" she pleaded.

I resisted the urge to say something mean like "An accurate impression," and slumped down the stairs to let in my mother's big date.

"You must be Guy," said Brad. He stuck out his hand and shook mine so hard that it hurt my knuckles. Buzz slid down the banister and landed between us.

"You must be Brad. I hear tell you're in fur," said Buzz, letting a little trace of his long-gone southern accent creep into the words so that he sounded friendlier than he was actually being.

"I am. And you would be—?" said Brad, extending his beefy hand toward Buzz.

"I would be Buzz," said Buzz, taking Brad's hand and shaking it vigorously.

Brad looked around uncomfortably.

"My mom'll be down in a minute," I said. "She's just putting on her, um, she's putting on her—"

"Particulars," said Buzz, jumping in to help me out.

I looked at him sideways. Particulars? Where the heck did *that* word come from? Still, he'd kept me from blabbing the truth about my mother's false eyelashes, something I'm sure she wouldn't have been anxious to have me share with this guy.

"No problem," said Brad with a wink and a smile. "How about a little something to wet my noodle while I wait for your mom?" he said, and winked again. Or maybe he wasn't winking—it might have been a nervous twitch. I tried not to stare.

"Wake up, Guy, and wet the man's noodle already," said Buzz, whacking me on the back.

"With what?" I asked.

"Whatcha got?" said Brad with yet another wink/twitch.

I led the way into the kitchen and pulled open the fridge. "Orange juice, seltzer, milk—"

"Anything hard?" asked Brad with—ooops! I looked away almost in time, but he managed to squeeze off another wink in my direction.

"Hard?" I asked.

"He means alcoholic," whispered Buzz.

"Oh, my parents don't drink," I said. "I mean, my mother doesn't."

"OJ is fine then," said Brad, and this time I made sure not to look at him.

I poured Brad some juice, then shot a few

ice cubes into the glass and handed it to him.

"What exactly does it mean to be 'in fur,' Brad?" asked Buzz in his sweet-as-pecan-pie voice.

"I'm a stretcher," said Brad.

"Excuse me?" said Buzz.

"A stretcher. I stretch the animal skins so they lie nice and flat when it comes time to piece the garments together," he said, and took a sip of juice.

I'd poured the orange juice into a Fred Flintstone glass we'd gotten for free from some fast-food joint. Fred was wearing a fur caveman suit, and I wondered whether Wilma had stretched the skins herself or if she'd had to hire some winking idiot with a bone-crushing handshake to do it.

"Well, helloooo," crooned my mother from the doorway. She was holding on to the doorframe and sticking one foot up in the air behind her, letting her high-heeled shoe dangle from her toe like an old-time movie actress. She had both sets of eyelashes glued on, and her eyelids were painted swimming-pool-bottom blue. The coffee cans had straightened her hair, which at the moment curved around her face like two stiff red parentheses.

"Hellooooo back at you, beautiful lady," said Brad. I noticed he didn't wink at her. Apparently that was something he saved just for us lucky kiddies.

Buzz and I rolled our eyes at each other.

"I see you've met the boys," said my mother.

"Yes, indeedy," he said. "So are you ready to push off, Lorraine from Spain?"

My mother giggled, and I figured it was up to her to set the record straight as to where she'd actually been born—Hoboken, New Jersey. It didn't rhyme with Lorraine, but it was a fact.

"Ready," she said. She pulled her blue

coat out of the hall closet and handed it to Brad, who held it for her while she slipped it on. Again I thought of the Christmas Day when my mother had opened the box that held that coat. She'd kissed my father on the lips for a long time. I'd thought it was icky at the time, but at the moment I would've given anything for things to be back the way they were then: the two of them together. The three of us together. Brad held the door open for my mother, but before she stepped out, she turned and said to me, "Why don't you and Buzzy order a pizza, okay, Guy?"

"Okay," I said.

"I won't be too late," she called from the porch.

I wasn't sure if I was supposed to say something to Brad like "Take good care of her," or "Drive carefully." I knew I wasn't supposed to say what was on the tip of my tongue at that moment: "She's married, you know, and they're going to be getting back together as soon as we figure out how to write the letter." So I just sort of waved at the two of them, and Buzz and I went back upstairs. I called up the pizza place and ordered a large pie with everything but anchovies.

"You know something, Guy?" Buzz said a little later, as we were polishing off the last of the pie. "I would seriously rather lie naked in the desert smeared with peanut butter and be pecked to death by hungry bald-headed buzzards than go out on a date with some goofy-acting female with huge flapping eyelashes and big shiny red lips—no offense to your mom."

"I know what you mean," I said. We took up our positions again, me leaning against the headboard and Buzz sitting cross-legged on the foot of the bed.

Then, without warning, the strangest thing happened. Autumn Hockney's face popped into my head. She smiled at me and flipped her long brown hair, and I was so surprised at the feeling it gave me in the pit of my stomach that I was momentarily tongue-tied.

CHAPTER SEVEN

We didn't make any progress with the letter at all that night, so we finally gave up and agreed to start fresh the next day after school. Since neither of us had any homework to do, we ended up watching the Westminster Dog Show on cable TV and laughing so hard that I got a terrible case of the hiccups, which just made us both laugh harder.

"What the heck *hic* is that, *hic*?" I asked, pointing at a bizarre dog whose fur looked like long black dreadlocks.

"Are you calling me a hick, boy?" said Buzz.

"*Hic.*" I laughed as the hiccup came at exactly the right moment.

"That's a puli, you ignorant bush pea. Don't you know *anything* about dogs?" he added in a snooty British accent.

"A puli, huh? *Hic.* Looks like a Rastafarian cocker spaniel, doesn't it?" I said.

"Hey, Guy, don't look now, but there's Autumn Hockney!" Buzz shouted, pointing at the screen excitedly.

"Where?" I said, jumping up and running over to the TV.

"There!" shouted Buzz with glee, pointing to a skinny Afghan hound with a pointy nose and long, shiny brown fur. The dog's owner led it around the ring on a leash while I collected myself and sat back down.

"Very funny," I said.

"Remind me to congratulate her on her Best of Breed blue ribbon tomorrow at school," said Buzz.

At least the shock of thinking that Autumn might be on TV had scared the hiccups right out of me. We watched until nine o'clock, and then Buzz headed home.

I had a dream about my father that night. He was wearing a suit coat and a big grass skirt and dancing a hula on a stage in front of a lot of people, including my mother, who was wearing the blue coat he gave her. I started running up the steps to the stage so I could talk to him, tell him how much I missed him, and ask him to come home. But the more steps I climbed, the more steps there were ahead of me. It was like trying to go the wrong direction on an escalator. I climbed so many steps that I ended up getting a terrible cramp in my leg, at which point I woke up with a real-life charley horse in my calf and lay in bed massaging it until my alarm went off at seven.

My mother was already downstairs making bacon. She looked like her old self again. Well, almost. Her eyelids were no longer blue, and her hair was curly again and pulled up on top of her head as usual, but instead of the rubber band or twist tie that she usually uses to secure it, there was a piece of brown fur clipped around the thick hunk of red frizz.

"Don't be alarmed, Mom, but I think there's a rodent in your hair," I said, sitting down and reaching for the milk to pour on my granola.

"That's no rodent, it's a mink barrette," she said as she touched the thing in her hair. "Brad gave it to me last night. What do you think?"

I just shook my head and jammed a big spoonful of cereal in my mouth.

In the lunchroom I saw Autumn carrying her tray across the room. She smiled at me and gave a little wave. I sort of smiled back and then went to sit with Buzz at our regular table.

"Did you see Bob-o this morning?" Buzz asked.

"Probably, but I don't remember. Why?" I said.

"He was hanging around in the hall with that Sabrina girl," Buzz said.

"Who's Sabrina?" I asked.

"You know, the one who wears those big glasses with the speckles in them."

"Oh yeah, I know who she is," I said.

"Well, look over there. See him? He's eating *lunch* with her," Buzz said.

"So?" I asked.

"Sheesh, Guy," he said with disgust. "It's practically like a date."

I turned around in my chair and watched as Bob-o leaned over and whispered something in Sabrina's ear. She let fly a high-pitched giggle and shot her paper straw wrapper in his face. It caught in his glasses, where it waved like a long, white antenna, and they both laughed as if that was about the funniest thing that had ever happened in the history of mankind.

"We're never gonna act stupid like that, are we, Guy?" Buzz said, throwing his arm over my shoulder. "How could we be friends if one of us started acting like an idiot, blowing around straw wrappers and junk?"

"You're not gonna stop being Bob-o's friend just because he's eating lunch with Sabrina, are you?" I asked.

"I'm not saying that. Look, he was a nose picker who kept rolled-up tuna fish balls in his pockets last year and we made friends with him anyway, right?" said Buzz.

It's true that Bob-o had come a long way since the year before, when Buzz and I had become completely convinced that Bob-o and I had been switched at birth. At the time I'd been horrified at the idea that he and I could be connected in any way whatsoever. Bob-o, to put it politely, has always marched to a different drummer. Sort of like my parents, or anyway my mother. His parents, on the other hand, are basically as normal and regular as apple pie. Sort of like me. It was hard not to jump to conclusions when we snooped around and found out that Bob-o and I had the same birthday, July fourteenth.

But in the end we figured out that we had each gone home with the right set of parents, and Buzz and I got to like Bob-o.

"You have to admit, he's a lot more normal now than he was last year," I said.

"Yeah, thanks to us. But now with this girl business . . . look at him." He pointed at Bob-o with a couple of disgusted jerks of his thumb. "I'm not so sure anymore."

"I don't see what's so bad about it," I said. "She seems like a nice-enough person."

"Sometimes you scare me, Guy. If I ever start acting like that, I want you to promise me right now that you'll do an intervention," Buzz said as he folded his peanut butter and jelly sandwich and took a big bite.

"What's an intervention?" I asked.

"That's like when people join weird cults and get goo-goo-eyed and nutty so their parents and all their friends have to go and kidnap them back, tie them to a kitchen chair, and unbrainwash them, " said Buzz.

"You know, I don't want to alarm you or

anything, Buzzeroo," I said carefully, "but there is a very good chance that eventually you're gonna think it's *normal* to like girls."

Buzz snorted, but I went ahead and finished my point.

"It doesn't have anything to do with brainwashing; it's something about hormones."

"Hormones, shmormones. There's nothing normal about acting like *that*," Buzz sneered as he pointed at Bob-o, who had stuck two straws onto his front teeth and was crossing his eyes and barking at Sabrina like a lovesick walrus, much to her delight.

I watched Bob-o and Sabrina carrying on with the straws for another minute. Then suddenly I flashed on my father, back in the old days when he was as weird as my mother, making his infamous pig face for her. He'd take a long piece of Scotch tape and use it to pull his nose and upper lip up into a strange piggy sneer by making loops in the ends of the tape and hooking them over his ears, then he'd chase her around the kitchen snorting and oinking like a fool. She loved it. He'd always been able to make her laugh. That was important, wasn't it?

I bet Brad wasn't the least bit amusing. Why couldn't my mother see that she was wasting her time going out with doofuses like him? Why wasn't she trying to get back together with my dad instead? He was so much better than any of these—

"Yoo-hoo. Anybody home in there?" Buzz said as he tapped on my temple with his index finger.

"Oh, sorry," I said, snapping back to reality. "I was just thinking."

"Again?" said Buzz. "You've been doing an awful lot of that lately."

"I've got stuff on my mind, okay?"

"Like what?" asked Buzz.

But before I could answer, someone tapped me on the shoulder.

"'Scuse me, um . . . Guy?" said a soft voice from behind me.

I swung around in my seat toward the

sound of the voice, and there she was—
Autumn Hockney, her braces glinting in the
sun, which streamed in through the lunchroom windows. She smiled and flipped her
long brown hair over her shoulders.

"Uh, hi," I managed to croak as I felt all
the blood rush out of my head.

Buzz let loose a deep, long rumbling
belch and then smiled at Autumn innocently.

"Repulsive," she said.

"Yes, you are." He smiled back.

I elbowed Buzz hard in the ribs.

"Hey!" he said. "What's the big deal? Just
a little air, that's all that was."

"Um, can I talk to you, Guy? Like, *alone*,"
Autumn said, looking me directly in the eye.

"We have no secrets from each other,
Hockney Puck. Anything you have to say to
Guy you can say in front of me. Right, Guy?"
Buzz said confidently.

"Well, um . . ." I stuttered, but then I was
literally saved by the bell. It rang for the end
of lunch period. Everybody shoved the last

of their lunches into their mouths and headed back to class.

Buzz went off to his study hall, and I took the back stairs up to the science lab on the third floor. I was a little nervous about Autumn Hockney wanting to talk to me alone. What was that all about? Was she going to ask me about going to the movies again? I still didn't know if I wanted to go. Why had I said "Maybe"? I should have just said "No," and then I wouldn't have to be worried about it now.

When I actually tried to picture it, Autumn and me at the movies, I was pretty sure it wasn't a good idea. What would we talk about before the movie started? What if her idea of a good movie was one of those cornball things I hate, with kissing and mushy love junk? I shuddered. Then I felt a tap on my shoulder. Oh, no. Not again. I held my breath and slowly turned around.

CHAPTER EIGHT

It wasn't Autumn—it was Bob-o Smith.

"Hey, Strang. I know something you don't know," said Bob-o as he smiled and pushed his glasses up his nose with his index finger.

"Oh, yeah? What do you know?" I asked. We walked together down the hall toward the lab.

Bob-o and I are science partners. A year ago I would have considered that a very bad stroke of luck, but now that we're friends, I don't mind working with him at all. He's actually very smart, and another big plus, especially in biology lab, is that he's not easily grossed out.

"I know someone who has a crush on

you," he said, and when he talked, I noticed he had a piece of lettuce stuck between his two front teeth.

"You've got green junk in your teeth," I said. "And how would you know who has a crush on me, anyway?"

"Sabrina told me," said Bob-o. He stuck his fingernail between his teeth and dislodged the lettuce. I was pretty sure I already knew who it was Sabrina was talking about, so I didn't really care when Mr. Blankman stood up in front of the class and told us all to clam up so he could tell us what the day's assignment was.

"Today we will be dissecting frogs," he announced in his high-pitched singsong voice.

The next hour passed very slowly. Each pair of students was given a big dead bull-frog and a dissection kit, which consisted of a pair of little scissors, tweezers, a scalpel, and a "frog board," which is a large square piece of Styrofoam that you're supposed to pin the frog down on before you cut it open. Even though Mr. Blankman kept saying we were doing it in the name of science, I felt guilty. Maybe a bullfrog's life isn't the most exciting life in the world, sitting around in pond muck eating bugs and all, but it had to be better than lying on your back while a bunch of kids who don't have a clue what they're doing go poking around in your guts with sharp instruments.

Out of respect for the dead, Bob-o gave our frog a name—Fred—but we ended up having to change it to Fredelle when we opened her up and found her absolutely stuffed with eggs.

"Aha, very interesting. You two have a gravid frog there," said Mr. Blankman. He had stopped by our table to check on the progress we were making with the dissection.

"Gravid?" said Bob-o.

"Pregnant," said Mr. Blankman, and then he walked on to the next table.

"Is this like caviar?" Bob-o asked, peering into the frog.

"I think that's only fish eggs," I said, "but if you want to spread some on a cracker and try it out, be my guest."

I filled in the worksheet as we went, identifying and checking off the heart, liver, esophagus, and stomach.

"What's that white stringy junk?" I asked Bob-o as we leaned over the frog board, our heads only inches apart.

"Fredelle's little intestines, I think," said Bob-o as he poked at them with the tweezers.

"Ish," I said. I checked off "intestines" on the worksheet.

"So, don't you want to know?" asked Bob-o, who was pulling a length of frog intestine out and holding it up to the light.

"Know what?" I said.

"Who has a crush on you," said Bob-o as he examined the disgusting stuff hanging from the tweezers.

"How can you think about that when you're up to your ears in frog guts, Bob-o?" I said, looking away from the swinging intestines.

"It's Autumn," said Bob-o. "Autumn Hockney thinks you're hot."

"Have you made an observation you'd like to share with the class, Mr. Smith?" boomed Mr. Blankman from right behind us. "You seem to have an awful lot to say to Mr. Strang today. Would you care to let the rest of us in on it?"

"I was, uh, just commenting on the lovely shade of pink some of these, uh, froggie innards are, Mr. Blankman. My . . . my . . . mother's got a bathrobe almost exactly the same color," Bob-o stammered.

Mr. Blankman harrumphed and moved away to another table, thank goodness. I could feel my face burning with embarrassment. It was bad enough knowing that he'd gone to the movies with my mother. But what if Mr. Blankman had heard what Bob-o was saying? What if he'd made Bob-o tell the whole class that Autumn Hockney had the hots for me? I couldn't wait for the bell to ring.

"So, Autumn Hockney. What do you think, Guy? Do you like her?" whispered Bob-o as we gathered up our dissection tools and notes and carried the frog board up to Mr. Blankman's desk for a final inspection of our work.

"Shut up, you moronic toadstool!" I hissed, praying that Mr. Blankman wouldn't notice Bob-o yammering away at me again.

"Well, do you?" he asked, undeterred by my name-calling.

I felt like I was being pursued by one of those yapping, nippy little dogs that take hold of your pant leg and won't let go.

"Drop the subject, will ya?" I said.

"But do you *like* her, Guy? Just tell me that," he said.

I had to get him to lay off—and fast—or I knew somehow Autumn's crush on me was going to end up being broadcast through the school like the freepin' six-o'clock news.

"What is your problem, Bob-o?" I said.

"I just want to know if you like—" he started, but I interrupted him.

"No! I can't stand her. Okay? I think she's a salamander. A drip. A gravid bullfrog. There, are you satisfied?" I said, hoping that would shut him up.

He looked surprised and a little bewildered, peering at me over the top of his glasses, but at least he was quiet. The bell rang, and I tossed the tools in the bucket of soapy water in the sink, washed my hands, and cut out of the classroom, leaving Bob-o still standing there by Mr. Blankman's desk, holding the frog board and what was left of poor Fredelle.

CHAPTER NINE

Buzz and I pushed through the heavy red double doors out into the rainy afternoon. It had been sunny that morning, so nobody had brought umbrellas or raincoats. Some kids carried their backpacks on their heads like lumpy makeshift rain hats; others were running home as fast as they could.

"Yo, Zuckerman!" shouted Buzz.

Lana Zuckerman, the tallest girl in the whole seventh grade, turned around when she heard her name. "What do you want, Doorbell Boy?" she called back.

"Nice raincoat," said Buzz.

"That's so lame it's not even an insult, so I'll take it as a compliment," she said.

Lana had torn a hole in the closed end of a black garbage bag and put the bag on over her head in an attempt to stay dry. She looked like a long shiny black sausage with feet as she hurried across the yard.

"Why does she call you Doorbell Boy?" I asked.

"Last year she called me Buzzer, so I just assume it's an updated version of the same thing. You know, doorbell, buzzer. Not the most clever nickname I've ever heard."

"Well, we can't all be as brilliant as you," I said as I pulled my collar up around my ears, hoping to keep the cold rain from dripping down the back of my neck.

"So did you get the stationery?" asked Buzz.

"What's the hurry? We haven't even figured out what we're going to say yet," I said.

"I know, but I think we should try to get the letter done today, don't you?" said Buzz.

"I still don't know if I think this is such a good—"

Buzz interrupted me. "Look, I think it's a great idea, right? And let's face it, we both know that I am much smarter about this sort of thing than you are."

"We do?" I said.

"Whose idea was it to have you and Bob-o switch places last year to figure out if you were really Bob-o and he was really you?"

"Wait a second. Are you trying to say that you think that was a *good* idea, Buzz? You must have forgotten that we ended up thinking that my mother had murdered Bob-o with a cake knife, and then you fainted dead away when he walked into the room. Remember?"

"The point is we figured out that you hadn't been switched, didn't we? That means it was a successful plan. Now we're on to the next mission—getting your dad and mom back together."

"I just don't know, Buzz, really."

"Trust me on this," he said.

We had reached my house. Even though

Buzz lives only a few blocks farther away, we never hang out at his house after school. In fact, I hardly ever go there at all. There's nothing wrong with his place. His mom and dad are perfectly nice and everything, but Buzz's room is really small, and his mom doesn't have anything sweet in the house on account of Buzz having so many cavities. Her idea of an after-school snack is carrots and rice cakes.

"Hi, Mom!" I called out as we came in the back door.

We took off our wet shoes and jackets, dropped our soggy backpacks in the corner, and went into the kitchen. Buzz headed right for the cookie jar, a big black-and-white ceramic cat from some ancient cartoon show my parents used to watch in the old days. We'd dropped the head so many times that his nose and both ears were missing, so he looked more like a snowman than a cat, but all that really mattered was what was inside.

"All reetie, baked ziti!" cried Buzz. "We've

got snicker doodles, ladies and gentlemen."
He held up one of my mother's famous
lumpy homemade cookies.

"Where'd that expression come from,
anyway?" I asked. I reached into the jar and
pulled out three cookies.

"Which expression? 'Ladies and gentlemen'?" asked Buzz, stuffing a whole cookie
into his mouth and reaching in for another.

"No, you gum wad, 'All reetie, baked ziti,'"
I said.

"Oh, that. I don't know. I've just always
said it."

My mom came in at that point. She
was blowing on her fingernails, which were
painted a shocking shade of luminous green.
"Hi, boys," she said. "You found the cookies?"

"Great snicker doodles, Mrs. Strang,"
said Buzz.

"What do you think, Guy—good color or
not?" my mother asked as she waved her
fingers in my direction.

"Looks like you stuck your fingers into

something nasty, like a giant's nose," I said.

"What do *you* think, Buzz?" she asked, ignoring my comment and turning to Buzz.

"Well, it's a very *interesting* color, Mrs. Strang. It sort of reminds me of creamed spinach," Buzz said.

"Yes, I see what you mean," she said, examining her fingernails carefully. "But is that good or bad?"

"That all depends on how you feel about creamed spinach," said Buzz.

"You're such a little diplomat, Buzzy," she said with a smile. "You, on the other hand," she said, pointing at me with one of her long green nails, "could use some lessons in manners from your friend here."

I thought about Buzz belching right in Autumn Hockney's face that afternoon.

"If you say so, Mom," I said with a little smile.

"Listen, boys. I've got a dentist appointment at three thirty. I have to leave right now, so can you please remember to turn on the oven at four o'clock? I've got a pot roast all ready to go in there. All you have to do is set it to 375° and turn it on."

"Okay, yeah," I said as I pulled another cookie out of the jar.

"Why don't you call your mom and ask her if it's okay for you to stay to dinner, Buzz? You don't want to miss out on my pot roast. But you have to promise me you guys won't forget about the oven," she said.

"You can depend on me, Mrs. Strang," said Buzz, giving my mother a crisp little salute as she hurried out the door.

"You can depend on me, Mrs. Strang," I said in a squeaky nasal voice. "What a kiss-up you are, Buzz. And tell the truth. What did you really think of that nail polish of hers?" I asked.

"Totally hideoso," said Buzz.

I laughed, and we headed up to my room. Buzz sat down on my bed, and I pulled a comic book off the shelf and flipped it open.

"Gimme that," said Buzz, snatching the comic out of my hands and tossing it on the floor. "No more stalling, Guy. We're gonna write that letter. Come on, get the paper."

"Okay, calm down," I said as I pulled the paper we'd used the night before out of my desk drawer and handed it to Buzz. "What do we have so far?"

Buzz read: "'Dear William.'" He stopped and put down the paper. "That's about it."

"Wow, that's an impressive piece of work there, huh?" I said.

"I'm going to ignore your lousy attitude and remind you that yesterday you suggested we make an outline of what we want to say in the letter," said Buzz. "So let's do that. What exactly is it that we want to say?"

"I don't know, Buzz. This is your bright idea. You tell me, what do we want to say?"

"Oh forget it," said Buzz. "I'm not going to lead you around by the nose like a piece of cheese."

"Like a *piece of cheese*?" I said.

We looked at each other and burst out laughing.

"I'm sorry," I said when I was finally able to catch my breath. "I know you're just trying to help, but I feel weird about impersonating my mother."

"It's only on paper. It's not like you're going to be walking around town in one of her dresses or something," said Buzz.

I pushed that ridiculous image out of my head and thought for a minute.

"Okay, what the letter needs to say is that no matter what's happened, she still loves him and misses him and wants him to come back, right?"

Buzz was writing furiously. "This is good, Guy. Keep going," he said.

"Okay, she should remind him about all the good times they've had together. Like picnics and barbecues and Christmas and Halloween. My parents love Halloween."

Halloween, wrote Buzz. "That's good. What else?" he asked, looking up at me.

"I don't know. Maybe she should remind him that they've had plenty of fights before and they've always gotten over them," I said.

"Uh-huh," said Buzz.

"And then I think she would probably say something about how I miss him too, and some junk about boys needing their fathers to be around."

"Yeah," Buzz said, looking up at me. "That's good. Anything else?"

"Do you think she should tell him she's sorry?" I said.

"For what?" Buzz asked.

"I don't know. She must have done something that made him mad, or he wouldn't have left."

"What did she do?" Buzz asked.

"I don't know. She makes me mad all the time. It could've been anything," I said.

"Well, it'll have to be a pretty vague apology then," Buzz said.

"How about something all-purpose, like, 'I'm really, really sorry for what I did, and I'll never do it again.' That works, doesn't it?"

"Works for me. Okay, here's the tricky

part. The ending. I've been thinking about this," said Buzz.

"What about it?" I asked.

"Well, I think we should say something like 'Please read this letter and then never mention it again.'"

"Why shouldn't he mention it again?" I asked.

"Because, you pollywog, if he mentions it to her, she's gonna tell him she didn't write it."

"Oh, right," I said.

"So let's put that in. Anything else?"

"Well, don't you think she should tell him she wants him to come home, since that's the whole reason we started doing this in the first place?" I said.

"Good point." He scribbled a few more lines. "Done."

We did the first draft on another sheet of notebook paper, and then I took a deep breath, and even though I felt bad about it, I went to my mother's desk and took out a sheet of her favorite paper—the stuff she had made herself with the papermaking kit my dad gave her for her birthday one year. The first few batches of paper she'd made had been disastrous because she'd tried to incorporate bits of red licorice, her favorite candy, into the paper since the instructions had said to personalize the paper by using bits of things that represent "the real you." The licorice got all gummy and made it impossible to write on the paper. The pen kept getting stuck in it. But my mother didn't give up, and the paper she eventually made, a piece of which I was in the process of swiping, had bits of flower petals and pine needles and stuff imbedded in it. It said *From the desk of Lorraine Strang* across the top. I carried it back to my room.

"We can't write this by hand. He'll know it's not her handwriting," I said.

"Can't you forge it?" asked Buzz.

"No way. Let's write it on the computer

and print it out on this paper," I said. "I think that'll work."

"Cool," said Buzz as he settled himself in front of the computer.

For someone who uses only two fingers when he types, Buzz is pretty fast. I dictated the letter to him from our final draft, making minor changes as we went. We ran the spell check and then inserted my mother's stationery into the printer and clicked on Print. The blue paper was just disappearing into the printer when my mother stuck her head in the door and said, "I thought I could trust you boys. How *could* you?"

uzz took two quick sidesteps, so that he ended up standing in front of the printer, blocking my mother's view of the emerging letter.

"Hey, Mrs. Strang. How the heck did it go at the old dentist, anyway?" he asked in a voice so loud that I cringed at the obvious false sound of it. "Did I ever tell you about the time I had five huge, gaping cavities in one visit and my mother said that if I ever—"

"Boys, how *could* you?" my mother said again.

Buzz stopped blithering and we both just stood there. Caught red-handed. Helplessly waiting for the printer to finish producing the undeniable evidence of our dishonesty. We held our breaths and waited for her to go over, pick up the letter, read it, and discover the full extent of our crime. Instead, she surprised us by saying, "Well, I guess we'll just have to make do with mushroom soup and saltines. It's hardly what I'd call dinner, but I should have known better than to trust the two of you distract-o-heads to remember to turn on the oven."

"Oh, the oven!" I said. "Buzz, we forgot to turn on the *oven*."

"Oh, silly us!" Buzz grinned at me as we both nearly fell over with relief.

"Sorry, Mrs. Strang."

"Yeah. Sorry, Mom," I added.

My mother raised one eyebrow at us, shook her head, and walked out.

"That was close," said Buzz as soon as she was gone.

"Too close," I said, reaching over and pulling the letter out of the printer.

"Let's get this thing finished up before

anything else happens," said Buzz. "You still gotta sign it."

"I don't know if I can make it look enough like her signature," I said.

"Do you have something to copy?" Buzz asked.

I yanked open my desk drawer and dug around in the junk. I pulled out a bunch of old stuff: a red-hot candy fireball, a couple of marbles, and a keychain I'd been looking for for months. Then I found what I was after, a stack of old letters and cards. I handed half of them to Buzz.

"Look through these for a good signature to copy," I said.

"Brilliant," said Buzz.

"Look, here's an old letter she wrote me at camp," I said.

"How'd she sign it?" asked Buzz, looking over my shoulder at the card.

"'Love, Mom,'" we both read out loud.

"I guess we could copy the 'Love' part, but I don't think she'd sign her letter to your dad from 'Mom,' do you?" asked Buzz.

"Nope," I said, and went back to looking through my pile.

After another minute Buzz said, "Bingo!" and held up an old valentine.

I took it from him and looked at the signature inside the card.

"No way, Buzz!" I said, handing it back to him.

"What do you mean? It's perfect," he said.

"I'm not doing it," I said.

"You have to," he said.

"Says who?"

"Okay, we'll draw straws. Short straw signs the letter," said Buzz. He tore two strips of paper from the back cover of my comic book. One long, one short. "Pick one," he said.

I considered carefully and chose the strip that was sticking up a little further out of Buzz's hand, figuring maybe he was trying to fool me into thinking that it was the short one. I was wrong. It *was* the short one.

"Aw, man," I said, crumpling the strip and tossing it onto the bed.

"Come on, what's the big deal?" Buzz said.

"If you feel that way about it, why don't *you* do it?" I said.

"Tell you what; let's both do it. Whoever does it better will sign the letter. Okay?"

"Okay," I said.

"So where does she keep it?" asked Buzz.

I grabbed the valentine and a sheet of blank white paper and led Buzz into the bathroom. We closed the door and stood in front of the medicine cabinet.

"Hey," said Buzz. "Since when are you taller than me?"

I looked in the mirror and was surprised to see that I was a good two inches taller than Buzz. "We used to be the same size, didn't we?" I asked.

"Yeah," said Buzz.

"Must be that strawberry-kiwi facial junk I ate the other day," I said. "Now, what do you think, pink or red?"

"Red," said Buzz.

I opened the medicine cabinet, took one of my mother's lipsticks off the shelf, and opened the tube. "I hate the way this stuff smells," I said.

"Yeah, me too," said Buzz.

We set the valentine on the edge of the sink so that we could copy the signature— a big lipstick kiss my mother had planted at the bottom of the card, right under where it said "BE MINE."

"How do you put it on?" asked Buzz.

"Like I know. I don't exactly make a habit of this, you know," I said.

Buzz took the metal tube and turned the end until the red lipstick stuck all the way out. "It's just like putting on Chap Stick, I guess," he said as he began to rub the lipstick vigorously across his lips.

"Whoa, slow down!" I said. "Chap Stick is invisible. This, on the other hand, is not. Look at yourself, you idiot."

Buzz looked at himself in the mirror.

"Sheesh," he said. "This better come off."

"It will," I said.

"Let me try making a kiss," Buzz said.

I handed him the piece of blank paper we'd brought in with us to practice on. Buzz put the paper to his lips and kissed it a couple of times. Then he studied the results.

"These stink. They look like red blobs. You can't even tell it's lips," he said, handing me the paper to look at.

"You're not doing it right," I said. "You need to pucker more."

"Since when are you the great kissing expert?" asked Buzz.

"I'm not saying I am. I just know that you're not doing it right," I said.

"Be my guest," said Buzz. He handed me the lipstick.

I looked in the mirror and tried to remember how my mother put on her lipstick. I'd watched her do it a million times. She moved her mouth around, puckering her lips and then pulling them tight over her teeth as she ran the lipstick slowly around her lips. I tried it and was amazed at how smoothly it went on. I overdid it a little on the corners of my mouth, but otherwise I managed to stay pretty much within the lines of my lips. When I finished, I blotted my lips on a piece of Kleenex the way she always does.

"Are you sure you never did this before?" asked Buzz.

"Shut up, monkey breath," I said. "Give me the practice sheet and let's try a kiss."

I kissed the paper and pulled it away from my mouth. A perfect kiss shape remained.

"Wow," said Buzz. "Awesome smooch, Strang."

"Think I'm ready to do the real one?" I asked.

"Sure, why not?" Buzz said, handing me the blue letter.

I carefully kissed the bottom of the sheet, then handed it to Buzz.

"Perfect, Guy Wire," said Buzz, examining my work.

"Good. Okay, now let's get this gunk off before my mother catches us again."

We scrubbed away at our lips with Kleenex and cotton balls, soap and water, toothpaste, shaving cream, and anything else we could think of that might fade the red stains. Although we managed to get most of it off, both of us looked a little pink around the mouth when we were done.

"How are we going to explain this to your mom?" asked Buzz when we finally emerged from the bathroom just in time to hear my mother calling us for supper.

"Don't worry, I'll handle it," I said, patting my front pants pocket. "Just follow my lead, Buzzy Boy."

We went downstairs and sat down at the table. My mother was ladling mushroom soup into three bowls. A plate of saltines and a dish of dill pickle slices were in the middle of the table.

"Holy smokes, what in the world have you two been up to?" she asked, looking at our stained mouths.

Buzz blushed and looked at me uncomfortably.

"Fireballs, Mom," I said. "Left over from Halloween."

"Oooh, I used to love fireballs. And I always did that same thing, ran them over my lips to try to rub off some of the really hot stuff so I could suck on them without burning my tongue. Do you have any left?"

"Yep," I said, glancing at Buzz as I reached into my front pocket. I tossed her the fireball I'd discovered in the drawer earlier when we'd been looking for my old letters.

"Thanks, Guy," she said. "I'll have it for dessert after this lovely so-called dinner."

"You know, soup is a perfectly respectable dinner, Mrs. Strang. And you make the best mushroom soup this side of the Mississip—"

My mother interrupted Buzz and looked at me. "Remember when I said you should take lessons in manners from Buzz?" she asked me.

"Yeah," I said.

"I take it back. I'm not sure I could stand all that buttering up. Makes me feel like a dinner roll."

We all laughed, and for the first time in a long time I felt pretty happy.

After dinner I walked Buzz to his house.

"So if you mail the letter special delivery, how long will it take to get there?" asked Buzz.

"I'm not sure," I said. "Couple of days maybe?"

"Hey, maybe you should fax it so we can get the ball moving right away," said Buzz.

"If I'd known we were gonna fax it, I wouldn't have bothered to swipe my mom's paper," I said.

"It'll still lend some authenticity to it. Remember, it does say 'From the desk of Lorraine Strang' on the top," said Buzz.

"Right," I said.

I dropped Buzz off, and on the way back to my house I stopped at the Mini-Mart, where they have a fax machine. It cost three bucks, half of my allowance, to fax the letter, but I didn't even think about it. It was a small price to pay for a chance at getting my family back together.

CHAPTER ELEVEN

The next morning at school I saw Autumn Hockney walking toward me in the hall when I was on my way to my locker to hang up my jacket. Before I could even begin to worry about whether she was going to come over and talk to me about going to the movies again, she turned around and walked quickly in the opposite direction. In Latin class she stared straight ahead the whole time and didn't even flip her hair.

Then at lunch something really weird happened. Buzz and I were just sitting down at our favorite table by the window when Lana Zuckerman walked by and made a mean face at me.

"What was that all about?" asked Buzz.

"I have no idea," I said.

Lana is Autumn's best friend. They always hang out after school, and they usually sit together at lunch at the big round table in the corner. I looked over, and sure enough, there they were. Autumn had her back to me, but Lana was looking right at me shooting darts out of her eyes in my direction. I quickly turned away.

"Girls are so whacked," said Buzz. "It's a waste of time to try to figure them out. They don't even know what they're thinking themselves half the time."

"Yeah," I said, but I couldn't help wondering what was going on. Had I done something to make Lana mad? Or Autumn? What could it be?

"So, did you fax the letter?" asked Buzz, changing the subject.

I felt a wet, stinging splat hit the back of my neck.

"Ouch!" I said, putting my hand up to the

spot. I pulled a little wad of wet paper off my neck.

"Spitball," said Buzz, examining it.

I turned around and looked for Lana. She was still sitting with Autumn, but she wasn't looking at me anymore. In fact, she almost seemed to be avoiding meeting my eye, and a mean little smile played at the corners of her mouth. There was no doubt in my mind that she was the one who had blown the spitball at me.

"I don't get it," I said.

"Girls," said Buzz with disgust.

The rest of that day was filled with strange events revolving around Autumn and Lana. Several more times I ran into Autumn in the hall, and she either turned around and walked away or walked by, pretending not to see me. Lana, on the other hand, seemed to be everywhere I went, and her presence was definitely not a ray of friendly sunshine.

Finally, on the walk home, it all came to a

head. Buzz had to stay after school to work on an art project for the school fair, so I was walking home alone. After a few blocks I was aware of someone walking behind me, but I didn't really think about it until I noticed that whoever it was, was kicking little pebbles up the sidewalk, and they were clipping me in the heels. I tried walking faster, but they just kept pace with me. Some of the pebbles got to be more like rocks, and finally one of them hit me in the back of the leg, and it really hurt.

"Okay, that's enough!" I shouted as I wheeled around to confront my tormentor.

No one was there.

"Lana Zuckerman, I know it's you. Come out here and face me—unless, of course you're too chicken," I said.

Lana stepped out of the bushes and put her hands on her hips. "Why would I be scared of puny, insignificant you, Guy Strang?" she said.

I couldn't think of any reason why she

would be; after all, she was a good head and a half taller than me and a whole lot meaner. So I just put my hands on my hips too and did my best to look tough.

"What's the problem, Lana? Why are you so ticked off at me?" I asked.

"Like you don't know. Autumn is my best friend, in case you hadn't noticed," she said.

"So?" I said.

"So don't be dense," she said.

"I'm not dense," I said, even though I felt totally dense at the moment. I had absolutely no idea what she was talking about.

"You owe Autumn an apology," said Lana.

"I do?" I said.

"Yes," she said. "And no more guy time. Got it?" And with that she turned on her heel and stomped down the street toward her house.

What had just happened? It was so confusing. Apparently I owed Autumn some sort of apology. But for what? And what was "guy time"? There was only one person I could think of who might know what it meant, and I wasn't at all sure it was a good idea to ask her.

"om?" I called as I came in the back door and headed for the kitchen.

"In here, honey," she called back to me from the living room.

I walked in and found my mother sitting on the floor surrounded by balls of yarn in every imaginable color. In the middle of it all was a mountain of little pieces of cut-up yarn, each one about three inches long.

"What are you doing?" I asked.

"I'm making a rug," she said. "I saw someone doing it on TV this morning, and it looked like fun."

"How are all those little pieces of yarn going to turn into a rug?" I asked. "You can't knit with those, can you? They're too short."

"It's a hooked rug. Like a shag, only this one is going to be unlike any other rug you've ever seen before."

"I believe it," I said, and I wasn't kidding.

My mother has made a lot of art projects over the years, and none of them ever look like anything anyone else would think to make. There was the watering can that she decorated by gluing old yo-yos all over it— some of which I would have liked to have held on to in their original working condition, by the way. And my lunchbox, which she covered with pictures of all things golf related even though I've never even held a golf club. These were two of her more useful artistic endeavors. The garage was filled with half-finished, less successful projects, like the rubber boots she melted holes in when she tried to hot-glue little packets of ketchup onto them. Or the lopsided sand castle we made in Nantucket one summer that she coated with layers and layers of high-gloss polyurethane in order to preserve it intact so we could lug it home in the back of the car and turn it into a coffee table.

"Do you need any help?" I asked.

My mother looked surprised. "You want to help me, Guy?"

"Sure," I said, sitting down next to her and picking up a ball of bright-blue yarn. "What do you want me to do?"

"Wrap that yarn around this little piece of cardboard twenty times and then cut both ends open like this," she said as she demonstrated on hers. It was a fast way of making a bunch of little pieces all the same length. We sat in silence for a few minutes wrapping and clipping yarn. Then I got up my nerve.

"Hey, Mom, can I ask you a question?" I said.

"Sure."

"Do you know what 'guy time' is?" I asked.

"Use it in a sentence," said my mom.

"Let's see. Um, 'You owe her an apology and no guy time, got it?'" I said, trying to remember how Lana had put it.

"Did someone say that to you?" she asked.

"Yeah. What does it mean?" I said.

"Who said it?" she asked. "And what are you apologizing for?"

"Someone said it for someone else who thinks I owe her an apology and I'm not even sure what for," I said. "But that's not the point. I just want to know what it means."

"Aha! You said you owe *her* an apology. So it's a girl," my mother said in this disgustingly sweet teasing voice she uses sometimes. "Someone special? Come on, Guysie. I'll tell you who I have a secret crush on if you tell me who your girlfriend is."

I should have trusted my instincts. Why had I asked my mother?

"I don't want to know who you've got a crush on," I said. "Just the thought of you having a crush on anyone makes me sick, Mom. All I asked you was if you knew what 'guy time' means."

"Come on, who is it? That girl who called the other night?" my mother asked. She was doing her usual thing, barreling along like a big pumpkin rolling down a hill, ignoring my feelings.

"I don't want to talk about it," I said.

"She sounded so sweet on the phone. But why do you have to apologize? Is she mad at you? What did you do?"

"I didn't do anything, Mom," I said as I stood up. "Can we just drop it?"

"What's her name, Guysie? Oh, I hope it's something romantic like . . ." She closed her eyes and waved her hands around in the air. "Felicity, or Rhapsody. Is it a lovely name like that?"

"Will you drop it already?" I said. I was really beginning to feel annoyed.

"See, the thing is," she went on, "you remember the name of your first true love for the rest of your life, so you don't want it to be something clunky like Gladys. Her name isn't Gladys, is it?"

"I don't know anyone named Gladys, and I never said anything about true love. All I asked is if you know what 'guy time'—"

"Oh Guy, you're blushing," she said, smiling up at me from the floor. "You don't need to get embarrassed. It's perfectly natural at your age."

"I'm not getting embarrassed. I'm getting mad. You just don't get it, do you? I'm not your friend, Mom. We're not buddies who sit around yakking about who we have crushes on. First of all, I don't have a crush on anyone. And second, even if I did, you're about the last person I'd tell. And third, in case you've forgotten, you're forty-three years old, and no matter how much fruit you smear on your face and how many stupid dates you go out on, that's not going to change. You're not the teenager around here, Mom, *I* am! So why don't you figure out what's *perfectly natural* for you to be doing at your age instead of trying to fool yourself into believing it's *perfectly natural* for you to be acting *my* age. It's *not!*" I was yelling by this point, and my mom looked like she was about to cry, so I dropped the ball of yarn I'd been squeezing in my hand and ran up to my room.

"Guy!" she called after me.

"Leave me alone!" I shouted back at her.

My mother called me down to dinner an hour or so later, but I pretended not to hear her. After a while she brought a tray up to my room.

"I know you're mad," she said, "but you still need to eat."

I was hungry, but I was too proud to admit it. So even though the meat loaf and baked potato sitting on the plate smelled so good my mouth watered, I didn't take a single bite.

Later, I lay in my bed with my stomach growling, feeling mad at the whole world. "Who can I turn to?" I asked myself. My mother was too silly to talk to, my father was probably sitting under a palm tree in his suit and tie having his nails polished, and Buzz, the only best friend I'd ever had, would have tied me to a kitchen chair if he'd known I was worrying about why some girl was mad at me. I felt completely alone.

CHAPTER THIRTEEN

"**A**ny word from your dad?" Buzz asked me the next day at lunch.

"Not yet," I said.

"Well, keep your antennas greased, okay? 'Cause I have a feeling that letter's gonna shake things up big time."

"Uh-oh," I said as I looked across the room.

"What's the matter?" asked Buzz. "Your lunch taste weird or something?"

"Oh, man," I said, watching Lana Zuckerman coming toward me with her lunch tray held out in front of her and an all-too-familiar mean look on her face. "This could be bad."

I knew she was up to no good, and sure enough, when she got about a foot away from me, she made a big deal about tripping over one of the chair legs. Then she very deliberately dumped her lunch tray right in my lap, splattering milk and macaroni and cheese all over my shirt.

"Yo, double-fault feet! What's your problem?" Buzz shouted, jumping to his feet and my defense.

"I'm *sooooo* sorry," Lana said in a fake sweet voice.

"What a bran muffin," Buzz said as he grabbed a couple of napkins and started to wipe the crud off the front of my shirt.

"Perhaps it would come off easier with a little water," said Lana, picking up a glass of water from the table and pouring the whole thing right in my lap.

"What is *with* you?" I yelled, jumping out of my chair. My pants were soaked, my shirt was a mess, and I was so mad, my ears were buzzing.

"Lana! What are you doing?" cried Autumn, who had come up behind her and was pulling her away from the table. "You're taking this way too far."

For the first time in days Autumn looked me in the eye. Well, first she looked at my wet, stained clothes and *then* she looked me in the eye. I thought she was going to say something, maybe explain what was going on. Instead, her eyes filled up with tears, she flipped her hair and grabbed Lana's arm, and she pulled her out of the lunchroom without a word.

When the bell rang, Buzz offered to stay and help me clean up, but I told him to go ahead on to class. I cleaned myself up as best I could, and then I went down to the office to call my mother.

"Mom?" I said into the phone. "I need you not to ask me any questions at all, just come pick me up as soon as possible. Please?"

My mother said okay. I signed out in the book in the office. The woman behind the desk took one look at me and didn't even ask why I was leaving. I went to wait for my mom by the front door.

She showed up about ten minutes later. I got into the car and did something I hadn't done in a long time. Burst into tears.

"Are you sick, honey? Did you throw up?" my mother asked as we pulled away from the school.

"No" was all I could manage to croak back at her.

We drove home in silence, except for my sniffling. My mother dug a crumpled tissue out of her pocket and handed it to me, and I blew my nose. When we turned up my driveway, I opened the car door before we had come to a complete stop, ran into the house, and went straight up to my room. I tore off my wet clothes and pulled on a pair of sweatpants and a T-shirt. Then I crawled under the covers and put the pillow on top of my head.

"Honey?" my mom said from the doorway.

"Do you want to talk about it?"

"No," I said from under the pillow.

"Well, if you change your mind, I'll be downstairs in the kitchen. I'm making cookies. Shall I bring you some when they come out?"

I didn't even answer her. I was too miserable to speak, let alone think about cookies. My mother went down to the kitchen, and I fell into a fitful sleep, the only thing I could think of to do to make this stupid nightmare of a day go away.

A couple of hours later I woke up in that hot, rumpled state you get into when you fall asleep in your clothes. At first I couldn't remember why I was home and asleep in my bed before it was even dark out, but then the lunchroom scene came tumbling back into my consciousness, and I groaned and pulled the pillow back over my head.

I tried, but I couldn't make myself go back to sleep, so I just lay there for a while trying not to think about the humiliating experience I'd been through. As I lay there, sounds from downstairs began to filter into my consciousness. I heard the kitchen timer go off. My mom clicking around the kitchen in her high heels. And there was a conversation going on. I recognized one of the voices—my mother's—but who was she talking to? Then I realized it was Buzz. Good old Buzz had come by to check on me. What a pal.

I pulled myself out of bed and went downstairs. The whole house smelled of fresh-baked cookies. I breathed in deeply, and for a second I actually felt a little better. Then I walked into the kitchen just in time to hear my mother saying, "He didn't give me all the details, Buzzy, but apparently this girl, I think it might be the one who called the other night when you were here, anyway, she's mad at Guy about something and demanding he give her an apology. He seems awfully upset about it."

I couldn't believe my ears.

"Mom! What are you doing?" I yelled as I rushed into the kitchen. "How dare you blab my private business all over the place? Isn't wrecking my home life enough for you—do you have to wreck my social life too?"

"Honey, I just assumed Buzz would know about your girl problems. Don't you tell each other everything?"

Buzz looked at me hard, and I could see that he was really hurt. "We used to tell each other everything, Mrs. Strang," he said quietly, as he pushed back his chair and got up. "But I guess that's all changed now." He walked across the kitchen and out the back door without saying good-bye.

For the second time that day I broke down and cried. I put my head on the table and sobbed. My mother tried to comfort me by patting my back, but I pushed her hand away. I hated her right then more than I ever had before. Hated her for blabbing my secret to Buzz, hated her for going out on dates with weirdos without ever considering how I felt about it, and most of all I hated her for blowing things with my father. I needed him right then. Needed him to talk to me, man to man. And where was he? Three thousand miles away, because of *her*. She'd probably done something horrible to him, blabbed something or ruined something important or done something unimaginably awful. Why did I have to have such an impossible mother? Why?

The phone rang, and my mom went to answer it. I felt a little glimmer of hope that maybe it was Buzz, calling from the corner phone booth to say he wasn't really mad at me, just a little hurt, and why didn't I hop on my bike and we'd ride out to the fort, the one we'd built the very first summer we'd been friends, and talk.

"It's for you, Guy," my mom said, holding the phone out to me.

"Is it Buzz?" I asked. I dried my eyes with the back of my hand and wiped my nose on my sleeve.

"No, it's your dad."

CHAPTER FOURTEEN

"**D**ad?" I said as I took the receiver from my mom and pressed it against my ear.

"Hey, Big Guy. How are ya?" said the far-away tinny voice on the other end of the line.

"Oh, just peachy," I said.

"Glad to hear it," said my dad, completely missing the sarcasm in my voice. "Listen, I've only got a minute, but I want to tell you something. Can you keep a secret?" he said.

"Sure," I said.

"I'm going to be in Cedar Springs tomorrow night."

"You're kidding me!" I shouted.

"What is it?" my mother said from behind me.

"Shh," said my father. "Don't tell your mother."

"What is it, Guy?" my mother said.

"Nothing, Mom. Dad just, um, uh . . ."

"Tell her I caught a really big fish," my father suggested quickly.

"Dad caught a really big fish, Mom," I said.

She shrugged and went to check the tray of cookies she had in the oven.

"When?" I asked.

"When what?" said my dad.

"When are you going on your next big fishing trip?" I said.

"What fishing trip?" he said.

"Dad, you were telling me about your trip *tomorrow night*. Remember? *What time* tomorrow night?" I said, trying my best to be clear to him and unclear to my mother at the same time.

"Oh, I gotcha now. You're asking me when will I be getting to Cedar Springs tomorrow night?" he said.

"Yes," I said. "What time tomorrow night?"

"I should be at your door at around nine o' clock," he said.

"How long will the, uh, *fishing trip* last?"

"Are you asking me how long I'm going to stay?" he asked.

"Yes, how long?" I said.

"That all depends," said my father.

I was about to ask him what it depended on, but then the intercom in his office buzzed, and I heard his assistant say that Mr. Somebody-or-other was waiting for him, and my dad said he'd be right there.

"I better go now, Guy. See you tomorrow. I can't wait to see you in the flesh."

"Me too," I said. He hung up.

My mother was looking at me funny, so I pretended my dad was still on the other end.

"Yeah, you have a good fishing trip now, okay, Dad? Catch another whopper. 'Bye."

I hung up the phone.

"What kind of fish did he catch?" my mother asked.

"Huh?" I said. "Oh, I don't know, like a

California trout or something, I think he said."

"Funny, I didn't even know your father liked to fish," she said.

But I wasn't listening. I was thinking about my dad coming home. I couldn't believe it. It must have been the letter. The letter had worked. I couldn't wait to tell Buzz. He would be overjoyed to know his plan had worked out. Then I remembered. Buzz was so mad at me right now, he probably couldn't care less about anything that had to do with my happiness.

"Guy, I owe you a big apology," my mother said.

"Forget it," I said.

"No really, I'm sorry," she said.

"It's okay," I said, even though I was still mad at her.

I had a hard time going to sleep that night. I kept thinking about seeing my dad and how good it would feel to hug him again. I thought about all the stuff I wanted to show him. My soccer trophy and my honor-roll certificate, and the skateboard I'd splurged on with my Christmas money. It was going to be great to have my dad back.

Right before I drifted off, I found myself wondering about two things my father had said. I wondered why he didn't want my mother to know he was coming, and I also wondered what he meant when I asked him if he was staying for long and he said, "That all depends." Maybe he wanted to surprise my mother by coming back and sweeping her off her feet or something, and maybe what his staying depended on was how she reacted to being swept. I closed my eyes and pictured my dad in a tuxedo and my mom in a flowy white dress—which wasn't all that easy since she almost never wears anything but stretch pants and the occasional table-cloth—dancing around the kitchen looking all happy and lovey-dovey. They were smiling and singing to each other like in a movie musical. Bubbles were floating through the air. It was a pretty great scene I cooked up, and I went to sleep with a smile on my face.

CHAPTER FIFTEEN

The next day at school was awful. If Autumn wasn't busy ignoring me, Buzz was. Lana was everywhere I looked, and she kept tapping her foot and looking at her watch like she was waiting for something from me. But what?

Only Bob-o would talk to me. I was standing behind him in the lunch line, pushing my tray along the counter. Neither of our mothers knows how to pack a decent lunch, so we both always get hot lunch. It's no great shakes, but it beats raw hot dogs and garlic knots, which my mother is under the impression is the same thing as a bologna sandwich.

"Can I eat with you today?" I asked.

"Sure. But how come?" he asked. "Is Buzz out sick?"

"No, he's mad at me," I said.

"Oh, that's too bad. Well, you're welcome to join me if you want, but you'll have to share me with Sabrina," he said, wiggling his eyebrows at me, which made his glasses jump up and down on his nose.

"That's okay," I said.

But when Sabrina came and sat down with us, she acted really funny toward me. Like it made her uncomfortable to be around me for some reason. Who knows, maybe I owed her an apology too.

"I guess she's used to having me all to herself," Bob-o whispered in my ear.

"Would you like me to go sit somewhere else?" I asked Sabrina.

"If you want to," she said.

Boy, I was about as popular as sour milk around this place. I picked up my tray and went to sit by myself at a small table by the door. No sooner had I sat down than Lana

Zuckerman plunked down in the empty seat next to me.

"I'm having one lousy day today, Lana," I said, "and I'm really not in the mood to be trashed by you again. So, since I'm already completely miserable, why don't you consider your job done and just leave me alone?"

"She's waiting," Lana said, looking at her watch.

"Who's waiting?" I asked.

"Autumn. Who do you think?"

Lana took one of the french fries off my plate and bit it in half with her sharp front teeth. I felt like I was watching some vicious predator, and I knew exactly who the prey was. Me.

"What exactly is she waiting for?" I asked.

"Do you need me to draw you a map?" said Lana.

"No, I need you, or better yet, somebody with a beating heart, to tell me what's going on."

"Do the words 'gravid bullfrog' mean anything to you?" said Lana.

I flashed back to the science lab and Mr. Blankman leaning over our frog board exclaiming over our egg-stuffed bullfrog, Fredelle.

"Yeah, *gravid* means 'pregnant.' Bob-o and I dissected a pregnant bullfrog," I said. "But what does that have to do with Autumn?"

"You've got a short memory, Strang," said Lana. "Do you remember using those two words to describe anything other than a dead frog? Like, for instance, *my best friend*?"

Suddenly I knew exactly what she was talking about. That day in the lab when Bob-o kept asking me if I liked Autumn, I'd blurted out a bunch of junk just to get him to shut up.

"I didn't mean anything by that," I said. "I just didn't want Mr. Blankman to hear what Bob-o was saying about Autumn having a crush— Hey, how did you know about that conversation, anyway? You weren't even there."

"I have my ways," Lana said, looking over her shoulder toward the corner table.

I followed her gaze and ran smack into Sabrina's blushing face. Bob-o must have repeated what I'd said about Autumn to Sabrina. No wonder Sabrina had seemed so uncomfortable with me around—she knew she'd gotten me in hot water.

"Why did Sabrina tell you about that?" I asked.

"'Cause she thought Autumn ought to know that the reason you hadn't called her back about going to the movies wasn't because of guy time, like she thought, but because you hate her guts and never intended to go with her in the first place," Lana said.

"What?" I said.

"Don't deny it. You told Bob-o you hated Autumn's guts."

"I may have said it, but I didn't mean it," I said.

"You didn't?" said a soft voice behind me.

I turned around, and there was Autumn.

She must have been standing there listening the whole time. She smiled a little and flipped her hair over her shoulder. I felt my whole face go red.

"I don't know what you see in this ripe tomato, Autumn, but I'm going to leave you two to work it out now. I've done everything I can," said Lana.

"I'll say," I muttered as Lana took another fry off my plate, shoved it in her mouth, and walked away, leaving Autumn and me alone.

CHAPTER SIXTEEN

"So you don't think I'm a gravid bull-frog?" said Autumn.

"No," I said. "But I think Bob-o is a gravid bullfrog. One of the large-mouthed varieties, to be specific."

"Don't blame him. He didn't even know what he was doing. Lana told Sabrina to snoop around and find out what was taking you so long. So she asked Bob-o to find out if you, you know, liked me. We were just trying to figure out if it was really guy time or something else."

"Stop right there. What the heck is this guy time I keep hearing about?" I asked.

"Waiting a really long time to let some-one know if you're going to the movies with them after you've said you'll get back to them is a classic example of guy time," she said.

"It is?" I said.

Autumn nodded.

"But it's only been a couple of days since you asked me," I said.

"Four," she said.

"Is that so many?" I asked.

She nodded again.

"Well, I'm kind of new to this stuff," I said. "I didn't realize there was a clock ticking."

"It's sort of an unofficial clock. See, I fig-ured if you really wanted to go, you'd call me back, like, the next day, and if you hadn't called me back by, like, two days after I called you, that probably meant you didn't want to go to the movies," Autumn said. "And after four days, well, I figured that was a def-inite no."

"Since we're being totally honest, I guess I should tell you that I didn't call you back because I wasn't sure how I felt about going to the movies with you," I said.

"Oh," she said, and she looked a little hurt.

"It has nothing to do with you," I added quickly. "I've just never gone to the movies with a, uh, girl before."

"Like I told you on the phone, Guy, there are a *bunch* of us going. Boys and girls. It's not like a date-date; my mother would have a cow if I even *thought* about going on a date-date until I'm at least fifteen. It's more like a group date. I just thought it would be nice if you came too. But if it makes you too uncomfortable . . ." Autumn said.

"What movie are you going to see?" I asked.

"*Warrior Bugs*," said Autumn.

"You're kidding," I said. "Really?" I was totally surprised. *Warrior Bugs* was this scary movie with giant spitting cockroaches and armed stinkbugs and junk. I was dying to see it, but I couldn't imagine Autumn wanting to sit there watching bugs decapitate each other.

"Yeah, I love all that gory stuff," she said.

"Really? Me too," I said.

"So why don't you come on Saturday? We're going to the three-o'clock show."

"Okay," I said. "I'll come."

"Really?" said Autumn.

"Sure," I said.

Autumn smiled a very wide smile that showed all of her braces. It was an impressive mouthful of metal.

"I'll see you Saturday then," she said. "Actually, I'll see you in Latin next period, but I'll see you Saturday too." She flipped her hair and walked away.

Well, that was one person who wasn't mad at me anymore. And since Autumn was happy, maybe Lana would lay off now. That just left Buzz.

CHAPTER SEVENTEEN

I waited for Buzz outside school for fifteen minutes after the final bell rang. I was just about to give up when he pushed through the red doors and started across the yard.

"Hey, wait up!" I called, but he didn't slow down.

I ran and caught up with him.

"Look, Buzz, I'm sorry I didn't tell you about what was going on. I was afraid you wouldn't understand."

Buzz kind of snorted, but he didn't say anything.

"You told me you'd tie me to a kitchen chair if I started liking girls, remember that?" I said.

"I remember," said Buzz. "I remember a lot of things. Like how my best friend never used to keep secrets from me."

"I would have told you eventually," I said.

"Yeah, right. Like maybe when you sent me the wedding invitation."

"Hold on a minute, Buzz Cut, you're blowing this way out of proportion. I'm only going to the movies with Autumn. That's it. And we're not going alone. A bunch of kids are going. I wasn't even sure I wanted to go at all, but then she told me they were gonna see *Warrior Bugs*," I said.

"*Warrior Bugs?*" said Buzz. "For real?"

"Yeah," I said.

"Cool. Still, you know you lied to me. You told me Autumn wanted help with her Latin," Buzz said.

"I lied about something else too," I said.

"You did? What?" asked Buzz.

"I told you I hadn't noticed that Autumn flips her hair," I said. "I noticed all right, and I kind of like it."

"If I had a kitchen chair here, you'd be in trouble, boy," said Buzz.

I felt this huge rush of relief. Buzz was joking with me, so it meant he was going to forgive me. "I'm really sorry I wasn't straight with you, Buzzy. I promise not to do that again," I said.

"Okay, I forgive you. You know what they say: Forgiveness is the next best thing to—to something, but I can't remember what it is right now."

I laughed and snagged Buzz's baseball hat by the brim, tossing it high into the air. He caught it and put it on backward. We grinned at each other, but then his face got real serious, and he said, "One thing though: If you really want me to forgive you, you're going to have to give me something."

"What?" I asked.

"Your Mark McGwire rookie card," Buzz said, looking me right in the eye.

Buzz knew that was my absolute favorite card in the world. I hesitated, but only for a second. "It's yours," I said.

"Sheesh, Guy. Are you nuts or something? I wouldn't take your Mark McGwire, don't you know that?" Buzz shook his head and turned his baseball hat around.

I have to admit I was relieved to hear it, but if it had been the only way to get Buzz back, I would have given up the card in a flash.

"Hey, what time is it?" I asked.

"Quarter to four, why? Got a hot date?" Buzz asked.

"As a matter of fact, I do. My dad's coming home at nine o'clock tonight," I said.

"All reetie, baked ziti; the letter *worked!*"

CHAPTER EIGHTEEN

Buzz came home with me. We came in the back way, stopped in the kitchen for some cookies, and then went up to my room. Or anyway, we started to go up to my room. Taped to the end of the staircase banister was a note that read:

> Guy:
>
> Gone to the horse show with Brad. Then dinner. Don't know when I'll be back. Leftovers in the microwave—just nuke them for five.
>
> —Mom

"Must be meat loaf. That's what we had last night. Want to split it with me?" I asked.

"Do you have a short memory?" asked Buzz.

"That's the second time today someone asked me that," I said. "What am I forgetting this time?"

"Your dad is coming home tonight. You don't have time to think about meat loaf. If you have any hope of getting your parents back together, we have to figure out a way to get your mom away from that horse show and winky-dink Brad and make sure she's home where she belongs when your dad gets here."

"You're right," I said. "But how are we going to do that?"

"Get the newspaper," said Buzz in his take-charge voice.

I got the paper, and Buzz flipped through it until he found what he was looking for.

"Okay, the horse show is at Metzgher's out on Route Forty-two. And here's the number. Write it down."

I wrote the number on a napkin. "Now what?" I said.

"Trust me on this, okay?" Buzz said.

Uh-oh. That made me nervous. Whenever Buzz says, "Trust me," it means he's about to suggest something outrageous. On the other hand, he'd told me to trust him about the letter to my dad, and it looked as if that had worked out perfectly.

"Okay, what do you want me to do?" I asked.

"You're going to have to tell a lie," Buzz said.

"Aw, Buzz, I don't want to do that. Look at the trouble it got me into with you. Can't we do something honest instead?"

"Okay, but remember, you asked for it," he said.

Buzz went over to the cabinet and pulled a jumbo-sized can of peaches off the shelf. "I'm doing this out of friendship, Guy Wire," he said.

"What? Making a pie?" I said, watching him walk toward me, holding the can over his head.

When he was standing right in front of me, he closed his eyes and dropped the heavy can directly on my foot. It hurt so much, I literally saw stars dancing in front of my eyes. I fell to the floor and grabbed my poor foot.

"Why did you do that?" I yelled. "It's broken."

"Well, I was going to have you *pretend* to be hurt—so that your mom would have to come home—but you said you didn't want to lie," said Buzz.

"Why did you listen to me?" I said.

"You don't really think it's broken, do you?" he asked quietly.

"It's starting to swell up," I said. I was trying hard not to cry, but it hurt so much, I wasn't sure if I could hold back the tears.

"I'm calling your mom," said Buzz. He dialed the number I'd written on the napkin and asked whoever answered the phone to page my mother. He told them it was an emergency, and a minute later he was talking to my mom. "Guy's had an accident," he said. "Something heavy fell on his foot. Actually, I dropped something heavy on his foot, and it looks pretty bad. . . . What? Oh, a can of peaches. It's kind of a long story. I think you better come home. . . . Okay. . . . Okay. . . . Okay. 'Bye."

"What did she say?" I asked.

"She said she'll be home in about fifteen minutes and that we should elevate your foot and put peas on it," said Buzz.

"Peas?" I said.

"Yeah, she said to get frozen peas out of the freezer and put them on your foot."

Buzz helped me hobble into the living room, where I lay down and put my foot on a stack of pillows he'd piled up on the end of the couch for me. Then he went out in the kitchen and brought back a big bag of frozen peas. He opened it up and poured them all over my foot. A bunch of them rolled off the pillows and onto the floor.

"Are you sure my mom said to use peas?" I asked.

"Yep," he said. "Is it helping?"

"Not yet," I said.

"I hope I didn't break anything, Guy," Buzz said. "Can you still move your toes?"

I tried to wiggle my toes, but it hurt, and besides that it made a whole lot more peas fall onto the floor. "I think I'll just keep it still for now," I said.

Buzz picked some peas up off the floor and put them back on my foot.

"I sure didn't mean to hurt you this bad, Guy," said Buzz.

"I'll be okay," I said. "And anyway, the important thing is everything is going according to plan now, right? My mom will be here when my dad gets home."

"Yeah, but there must have been a better way," he said, looking sadly at my foot poking out from under the peas. I could tell he felt terrible.

"It's okay, Buzz Cut," I said. "Just promise me next time you'll use a smaller can of peaches."

"Or better yet, a bag of marshmallows," he said.

A little while later we heard a car in the driveway. My mother came running into the house, calling my name. When she saw me lying on the couch, she came rushing over, all concerned. Then she stopped.

"Why are there peas all over the place?" she asked.

"You told me to put peas on his foot, Mrs. Strang. Remember?" said Buzz.

"I told you to put a *bag* of frozen peas on his foot, Buzzy."

"I did. That's the whole bag," he said.

"I can see that," she said. "The thing is, it works just as well and it's a lot less messy if you leave the peas in the bag."

"Oh," said Buzz. "Sorry."

"Doesn't matter. Let me see the foot, Guysie." My mom pushed some of the peas off my foot and looked at it. "Oh, you poor baby, it's turning purple. I wonder if we need to get an X ray. I'd better call the doctor. Do you want a Tylenol?"

She brought me a glass of water and a couple of Tylenol. Then she went to call the doctor. While she was on the phone, there was a knock at the door.

Buzz and I looked at each other.

"What time is it?" I asked.

"It's only five thirty," I said.

"Maybe he caught an earlier flight," Buzz said.

"Go let him in," I said, sitting up on one elbow so I could see my dad when Buzz opened the door. "Hurry up!"

"Welcome home, Mr.—" Buzz stopped in midsentence.

"Howdy-do! Good to see you again—

wait, don't tell me—Bizz. That's your name, isn't it? Bizz. I've got a memory like a steel trap."

Brad walked past Buzz and came on into the living room. He looked at me and then at the pea-strewn floor. "I thought your mother said it was a can of peaches that fell on your foot. Looks like peas to me," he said. "So how's the patient?" he asked.

I noticed he hadn't winked at me once since he'd arrived. I guess he felt winking at someone who was in pain was inappropriate.

"Doctor Davidson says we need to get it x-rayed," my mother announced as she came into the room holding my jacket in her hand. "We're going to meet her over at the hospital. Let's go."

"I'll drive you," said Brad. "I can't provide a spinning cherry on top, but if you want me to, I can open my window and wail like a siren."

I looked at Buzz.

"Can I come along, Mrs. Strang?" he asked.

"Of course," said my mother.

Well, so much for things going according to plan.

CHAPTER NINETEEN

It took three hours to get my foot x-rayed. Most of that time was spent sitting in the waiting room. Buzz and I passed the time by playing our own version of I spy.

"I spy something ridiculous," Buzz said.

"Brad's fur belt buckle?" I guessed.

"Right-o. Your turn."

"Okay, I spy something even more ridiculous," I said.

"Brad's fur wallet on a chain?" Buzz guessed.

It helped pass the time, and it also helped keep my mind off my foot, which had swollen quite a bit by then and was throbbing like crazy.

The X rays revealed that one tiny bone in the top of my foot had been fractured by the can of peaches. Dr. Davidson put a soft cast on my foot, and I left the hospital on a pair of crutches.

"I feel terrible," Buzz said to me as he held my crutches while I slid into Brad's backseat. "Is there anything I can do to make up for this?"

"Yeah, make sure Brad doesn't come in when we get to my house. It's eight thirty. If we get rid of him, then my mom can still be where she's supposed to be when Dad gets there, and all of this won't be for nothing."

"You can count on me," said Buzz.

When we pulled up to my house, Brad turned off the car and started to get out, but Buzz jumped right in and said it would be really so great if he could drive Buzz home, and if it was all right with him could they please, please stop at the Mini-Mart on the way because his mom had asked him to pick up some milk. Brad said okay and then asked my mom if she wanted him to come back after he dropped Buzz off.

"No, no, that's okay, Brad. I'll call you later. Thank you for all your help. And I'm sorry we made you miss most of the horse show."

"No problem. You take care of that foot now, Guy," he said, and he squeezed off a great big fat wink in my direction. I thanked Brad for the ride and gave Buzz a thumbs-up sign for getting him out of the way in a hurry. Then my mom and I made our way up the driveway and into the house.

My father was sitting at the kitchen table, his shirtsleeves rolled up and his tie flipped back over one shoulder, eating a bowl of peaches. "I hope you don't mind," he said, pointing to the peaches. "I was starved after the long flight."

CHAPTER TWENTY

My mother was pretty surprised to see my father sitting there in the kitchen.

"William? What in the world—" she said.

"Dad!" I shouted.

I hobbled over and hugged him as best I could, what with the crutches and my sore foot and all.

"What happened to you?" my dad asked as soon as we stopped hugging.

I told him about the can of peaches falling on my foot.

"And here I am eating all the evidence," said my father. "I hope you weren't planning to sue."

I laughed and hugged my dad again. It was so good to see him.

"You know, Guy," my mother said, "I don't think I ever asked you—what was Buzz doing with that big can of peaches in the first place?"

"I think he said something about wanting to make a pie," I said. I wasn't about to tell her it had all been part of a big plot to make sure the fur man wasn't around when my dad got home.

"Huh. I didn't know Buzz had any interest in baking," she said.

A sort of uncomfortable silence settled over the room.

"So, I understand you've become quite the fisherman," my mom finally said.

"Fisherman? Who, me?" my dad said.

"Remember, Dad? We made that up so you could surprise Mom when you showed up tonight," I said.

"Surprise me?" my mother said.

"Well, you're surprised, aren't you?" I said.

"You could say that. I mean, I certainly wasn't expecting to find you sitting in my kitchen eating peaches tonight," she said to my father.

What did she mean, *her* kitchen? Since when was it *her* kitchen? Here I'd gone to all this trouble to get my dad to come back, he'd flown thousands of miles to get here, and she was starting in already, acting crummy and unfriendly. I wasn't about to let her blow this.

"Hold on. It's not just *your* kitchen, Mom. It's my kitchen too, and my kitchen is your kitchen, Dad. You can eat all the peaches you want as far as I'm concerned," I said.

My father ate a mouthful of peaches and reached over to rumple my hair.

"So, how shall I put this—what brings you to *Guy's* kitchen, William?" my mother said.

"I'm sorry if my being here comes as an

unpleasant surprise, Lorraine. I didn't want Guy to tell you I was coming because I thought, well, to tell you the truth, I thought you might tell me not to, and there's something important I really need to talk to you about," he said.

They both looked at me, and I could tell that was my cue to leave the room.

"I think I'll go up and get ready for bed. I'm pretty zonked," I said.

"I'll come up and tuck you in a little later, okay, Guy?" said my dad.

I hadn't needed to be tucked in for years, but I was so glad to have my dad back that I would have let him sing me a lullaby if he'd wanted to.

"Can you manage the stairs alone, honey?" my mom asked as I made my way across the room on my crutches.

"I think so," I said.

"Guy?" my mom said. "I meant to tell you—I'm glad you and Buzz made up."

"Were you fighting with Buzz?" my dad asked.

"Yeah, he was mad at me about something, but he forgave me."

"That's good," said my dad.

"Yeah, you know what they say about forgiveness," I said. "It's the next best thing to, um, to . . ."

"A grapefruit in the head?" my father said.

My mother surprised me by laughing out loud at that and snapping the kitchen towel at my father—something she used to do all the time back when she liked him.

"I'm glad to see all that California sunshine hasn't dried up your sense of humor," she said.

It seemed like the perfect time for me to cut out of there. My parents were smiling at each other, and, who knew, maybe I wasn't the only one who was going to be forgiven that day.

"Good night," I said, and went upstairs.

My mother blew me a kiss, and my dad said, "I'll be up in a bit."

I brushed my teeth, put on my pajamas, and got into bed. It was a little hard to get comfortable with the cast under the covers, so I folded back the covers and rested my foot on top of the blankets. As I lay there waiting for my dad to come up, I listened to the murmur of my parents' voices down in the kitchen. It was a wonderfully familiar, comfortable sound, like crickets in the summertime or the muffled sound of traffic when the roads are snowy. Plates and silverware clinked; my mother was probably making my dad something to eat while they talked. I wondered what they were talking about. I hoped he was telling her that he wanted to come home and that he forgave her for whatever it was that she'd done. And I hoped that she was saying "Yes, please do come home, we've missed you so much."

I crossed my fingers, each one over the

next, the way I'd done when I was little and wanted something really, really badly.

I must have fallen asleep while I was waiting for my dad, because when I woke up, the sun was streaming in my window. It was morning. I started to jump out of bed, but a sharp pain in my foot reminded me that jumping out of bed was not going to be an option for me for quite a while.

"Dad?" I called from my room as I carefully got up and reached for the crutches I'd left leaning against the chair. There was a note from my dad taped to one of my crutches.

> Guysie:
>   You were sound asleep when I came up. See you tomorrow.
>   XXOO
>
>   Dad

"Your dad's not here right now, Guy," my mother called from the bottom of the stairs.

"Come on down here, will you? I want to talk to you."

I hopped down the stairs on my good foot and then used the crutches to get to the kitchen. My mother was making home-made waffles in the waffle iron. A bowl of cut-up strawberries and a can of whipped cream sat on the counter.

"Mmm, my favorite," I said. "Are we cele-brating something?"

Please, please, please, I chanted to myself, *please tell me that he's coming home for good.*

"We could celebrate your broken foot," she said.

"Can't you come up with something a little better than that to celebrate?" I asked.

Please, please, please, tell me that he's com-ing home for good.

"Guy, we need to talk about the letter," my mom said.

"What letter?" I asked.

"The letter you wrote to Dad," she said as she put a plate of waffles down at my place, took my crutches, and helped me sit down.

"How did you know that I wrote it?" I asked.

"There were several little tip-offs. My guess, based on some of the language you used, is that Buzz had a hand in this too. But what we need to talk about right now is the apology," she said.

"Which apology?" I asked. There had been so many in the past few days, I wasn't sure which one she meant.

She pulled the letter I'd faxed to my father out of her apron pocket and unfolded it slowly. Then she read it out loud:

"'Dear William,' blah, blah, blah . . . here it is: 'I'm really, really sorry and I'll never do it again.'"

"What about it?" I asked.

"Guy, what makes you think that I did something for which I owe your dad an apology?"

"I don't know. I figured you must have

done something to make him mad or he wouldn't have left. So I thought maybe if you said you were sorry, Dad would come home."

"Guysie, I know you mean well, but you're in way over your head here."

"What does that mean?" I asked.

"It means that what's happened between your dad and me is a lot more complicated than you could possibly understand."

"How complicated could it be just to say you're sorry? I did it with Buzz."

"I know you did, and I'm proud of you for doing it. But what you have to understand is that I didn't do something to your father to make him mad and make him want to go away, and he hasn't been hanging around in San Diego waiting for me to cough up an apology. He changed, Guy. A lot. And I didn't. We weren't happy together anymore, either one of us, so we decided *together* that the best thing for us to do was to separate."

"Well, it's not the best thing for me."

"I know, Guy, and I'm sorry that this has happened to you. Your dad is sorry too. Your letter made him realize how hard this has been on you, and that's why he came back. Why he's coming back."

"Coming back? You mean, for good?" I asked as my heart suddenly pounded in my ears.

"Yes and no," she said. "He's coming back to live in Cedar Springs, but he's not moving back in with us. He's with a realtor right now looking at a house just a few blocks from here. He wants to spend as much time with you as possible, but we're still going to go through with the divorce, honey."

I vowed never to cross my fingers and wish for anything again, because it clearly didn't work worth beans. My family was just as busted up as ever, and it didn't look like things were ever going to go back to the way they'd been before. I pushed my untouched waffles away, folded my arms on the table, and put my head down on them.

"I know you're disappointed, and I know how hard this has been on you," my mom said.

"No, you don't," I said.

"Then tell me," she said.

Those words were like a key turning in a lock deep inside me. *Tell me.* Suddenly all the things I'd been keeping hidden inside came pouring out. I told her how much it had bothered me when she'd gone out with Mr. Blankman, and how it hurt my feelings when she forgot to make cookies because she was too busy getting ready for one of her dates. I told her how I worried every time she went out with someone new that she might end up marrying him and I'd have to get used to having a new father when all I wanted was my old father back where he belonged. I told her that it was hard enough to be dealing with my social life without her teasing me and asking me questions I didn't want to answer. The more I told her, the lighter I felt. It was as if I had been carrying a heavy pack on my back for a long, long time and now I was finally slipping it off my aching shoulders. My mother sat quietly and listened to me, and when I was finally finished, she said, "I wish you had told me all of this earlier, Guy."

"I wanted to, but it just took me a while to find the right time. Probably 'cause I'm a guy," I said.

"Huh?" said my mom.

"*Guy time*, remember?" I said.

"Oh, *guy time*. Right. I never answered your question about that, did I? I'm sorry," she said.

"That's okay, Mom, I figured it out on my own," I said. "Well, actually my friend, um, Autumn told me."

"Autumn? That's a beautiful name."

"Beats Gladys," I said.

My mother smiled.

"Anyway, Autumn told me that *guy time* is when a guy takes his sweet time letting somebody, usually a girl, know what he thinks or feels about something."

"Sounds like a good definition to me," said my mother. "But you know, I don't think you can chalk it up to guy time in this case. I should have been paying more attention. I've been so caught up in my own feelings, I haven't been paying enough attention to yours. I'm sorry," she said.

"If I have to say or hear 'I'm sorry' one more time this week, I'm gonna puke," I said, "No more apologies. Deal?"

"Deal," she said. "But I can't speak for your dad. He feels terrible. He knew he shouldn't be staying in California for so long. It just took him a long time to get it together to come home."

"Guy time, right?" I said. "Maybe it's hereditary."

"You're funny," my mother said with a laugh. "Anyway, your dad and I had a good talk last night. We're still friends in a lot of ways, Guy. And we both love you more than anything in the world."

"I just wish . . ."

"I know, honey. I know. But you'll see. With your dad in town, it won't be exactly the way it was before, but it'll be a lot closer."

"I guess," I said.

She leaned over and put her arms around me. I closed my eyes and laid my cheek on her shoulder. And I let her hold me, rocking gently, back and forth, for a long time.

CHAPTER TWENTY-ONE

We bought a big tub of buttered popcorn to share and two Cokes. Autumn paid for half of it. She got two straws and stuck them in my shirt pocket along with a couple of napkins. Then she carried the drinks and the popcorn, because I had my hands full dealing with the crutches. A bunch of kids from school, including Bob-o and Sabrina, were sitting in a row right smack in the middle of the theater. There were a few seats left on the end, so I let Autumn go in first, and then I sat down in the seat next to hers, being very careful not to accidentally touch her at all as I pulled my sweater off and sat down. My palms were a little sweaty and my mouth was dry, but I kept telling myself, *What's the big deal? She's just here to watch a movie, the same as you are. . . . You've sat in a movie theater next to a girl before—just not on purpose. . . .*

Autumn and I reached for the popcorn at the same time. "After you," I said.

She smiled, flipped her hair, and took a handful of popcorn. "I'm not allowed to eat this because of my braces," she said.

"It's probably not good for broken bones either, but I won't tell if you won't," I said as I took a handful for myself.

Bob-o shot his straw wrapper down the row and got me right in the ear. I shot mine back at him and scored a bull's-eye right between the eyes. Autumn had been right about him—he'd had no idea that he'd gotten me in trouble by repeating what I'd said to him in the lab—so I couldn't really stay mad at him.

Autumn laughed as the straw wrappers

flew. Then she reached into the tub and took more popcorn. I was surprised at how easy it was to be with her. In fact, it almost felt normal. The lights started to dim, and I heard a familiar voice coming from somewhere behind us in the theater.

"Watch where you're going, will ya? It's dark in here, in case you haven't noticed."

Two shadowy figures appeared in the aisle near us—a boy and a girl. The girl was considerably taller than the boy was, and as I watched, she stuck out her foot and tripped him on purpose. He stumbled, and popcorn flew up in the air and rained down all around us.

"I'm sooooo sorry," she said.

He laughed and punched her in the arm. "You have a twisted sense of humor, you know that?" he said.

The girl picked a piece of popcorn out of the boy's hair. She tossed it high up in the air and caught it in her mouth.

"All reetie, baked ziti!" he exclaimed.

"Buzz?" I said, not quite able to believe it. But it really was Buzz. And the tall girl with him, I was totally shocked to see as my eyes adjusted to the dark, was none other than Lana Zuckerman.

"*Psst.* Guy Wire, are you guys in here somewhere? Give me a sign," said Buzz in a loud whisper.

"Over here," I whispered back, and waved my hands in the air so he could see me better.

Buzz and Lana slid into our row and sat down in the last two empty seats next to me. "Mind if we join you?" he said as he took off his jacket and put it over the seat behind him.

"*We?*" I said.

"What can I tell ya? Lana called me this afternoon and asked me to come to the movies with her, and I figured—if you can handle it, so can I, right?"

I was so surprised, I didn't know what to say.

"Hi, Autumn," Buzz said, giving her a little wave.

"Don't you mean *Hockney Puck?*" said Autumn.

"Truthfully, I think it's one of the most clever nicknames I've ever come up with. If you want me to call you that, I will, but I think Autumn is a beautiful name," said Buzz.

Autumn looked at me and shrugged. "What's with him?" she asked.

"He's being charming," I said. "My mother says it makes her feel like a buttered dinner roll."

Autumn laughed and took a sip of her Coke.

"Hey, Lana," said Buzz, "what's that on your shirt?"

Lana looked down at the front of her shirt and Buzz tweaked the end of her nose with his finger. I couldn't believe what I was witnessing: Buzz was flirting with a girl.

I leaned over and whispered in his ear. "After the movie I want you to come over to my house. There's a kitchen chair I'd like you to sit in."

He laughed and rolled his eyes at me. As the coming attractions flashed onto the screen, I closed my eyes, slid down in my seat, and leaned my head back for a minute. With the bright lights flickering through my eyelids, I took a deep breath and thought about how I felt—pretty good, considering I had a broken foot and my parents weren't getting back together. I guess that's one of those funny things about life. You walk around thinking you can't be happy unless everything is perfect, but then one day you realize maybe you can.

Autumn tapped me gently on the shoulder. I opened my eyes and looked at her.

"You okay?" she whispered.

"I'm fine," I said.

She smiled and flipped her hair, and then we turned our attention to the giant stag beetles eating the opening credits and spitting out the mangled letters like machine guns.

"This is gonna be great," Buzz whispered in my ear.

"Yeah," I said. "It is."

The fun continues in

ARAH W   K'

next book

MY GUY

Here's a peek:

"I knew this was going to happen. I just knew it," I said when Buzz and I met on the corner to walk to school together.

"What?" he said, yanking up his sleeve to look at his watch. "Am I late?"

"I'm not talking about punctuality, you cornflake. I'm talking about life and death."

"Well, I'm glad *you* know what you're talking about, Guy, because I sure don't."

I didn't see any point in beating around the bush. Buzz is my best friend, and I tell him everything. Even the awful stuff. Like this horrible piece of news.

"My mother is getting married," I said.

Buzz stopped in his tracks and turned to

look at me. "*What?* Oh, man. Please tell me she isn't gonna marry that dork Brad."

"No," I said. "Worse than Brad."

"Come on. Who could be worse than Brad?" asked Buzz. "The man winks and has a wallet made out of fur."

"Trust me, *Jerry* is worse than Brad," I said.

"Who's Jerry?"

"Jerry Zuckerman." I kicked a stone on the sidewalk and sent it skipping out into the street.

"Who's Jerry Zuckerman?"

"*Zuckerman*, you trout. Does it ring a bell?" I said.

"Not really," said Buzz. "The only Zuckerman I know is Lana."

"Exactly."

"Exactly what?" he asked.

"Jerry Zuckerman is Lana Zuckerman's father."

Buzz screwed up his face in disbelief.

"Your mother is marrying *our* Lana Zuckerman's father?"

I nodded.

"Sheesh," Buzz said with appropriate feeling.

I've known Lana Zuckerman since kindergarten, when she used to torture me by calling me "Girlie Guy" because of the pink mittens my mother made me for Christmas that year.

"Pink is a girl's color," I said with utter dismay as I stared at the mittens on Christmas morning.

"Oh, pooh," my mother said. "How can someone own a color? Look at your skin, Guysie. It's pink. And you're a boy, aren't you? That pink and blue business is just nonsense. I don't believe in it."

Well, I believed in it, and apparently so did Lana Zuckerman and the rest of the kids in her crowd. The day I wore those mittens to school, they chased me around the playground yelling, "Girlie Guy! Girlie Guy! Let's have a tea party!" until finally the teacher came out and called them off. I accidentally "lost" the mittens down the sewer grate on the way home from school that day. But losing the unpleasant memory has proved to be a lot harder.

From kindergarten on, somehow Lana and I ended up in the same class every year until we went to middle school. She was always the tallest kid in the class, boy or girl. She towered over everyone, and anyone who tangled with her once knew enough to avoid doing it again. She's as mean as a snake and about equally appealing.